The Block

The Block

Treasure Hernandez

www.urbanbooks.net

Urban Books, LLC
78 East Industry Court
Deer Park, NY 11729

ISBN 13: 978-1-60162-497-0
ISBN 10: 1-60162-497-2

First Printing May 2012
Printed in the United States of America

10 9 8 7 6 5 4 3 2 1

This is a work of fiction. Any references or similarities to actual events, real people, living, or dead, or to real locales are intended to give the novel a sense of reality. Any similarity in other names, characters, places, and incidents is entirely coincidental.

Distributed by Kensington Publishing Corp.
Submit Wholesale Orders to:
Kensington Publishing Corp.
C/O Penguin Group (USA) Inc.
Attention: Order Processing
405 Murray Hill Parkway
East Rutherford, NJ 07073-2316
Phone: 1-800-526-0275
Fax: 1-800-227-9604

The Block

Treasure Hernandez

Chapter 1

Tone sat in the passenger seat of the new Audi staring blankly out the window, stuck in his own thoughts, while his main man Maine drove. Tonight was no different from any other night. Tone had just got word on some guy named Sam that owed him some money, and he was going to make sure the man paid up. Tone was the leader of the empire that he was building from the ground up, and everybody knew he and his crew didn't play, so for Sam to be trying to duck him didn't sit well with him not one bit.

Maine pulled up in the empty parking lot and saw Sam surrounded by twelve of Tone's goons. "That's him right there?" he asked.

"Yeah, that's that nigga," Tone said in a cool tone as he stepped out the Audi, a bottle of Grey Goose in his hand. He was angry that Sam was trying to duck him, but even more so that he had to leave the comfort of his home to come out here right now. He passed the bottle of Grey Goose over to Maine as he walked up to Sam.

"Yo, fam, where's the rest of my money at?" Tone asked in a cool tone.

Sam looked at Tone and the twelve goons he had standing behind him and took a deep breath. "I got robbed," he replied, a look of shame on his face.

"Got robbed?" Tone echoed. "Fuck you mean, you got robbed? Who robbed you?"

"Gruff and that bitch Maxine," Sam answered.

Tone let out a deep breath as he turned and smacked the shit outta Sam. "Nigga, you let a nigga and a bitch rob you?"

"Nah, son, that nigga Gruff—"

"Nigga, shut the fuck up!" Tone said, quickly cutting Sam off. "Empty ya mu'fuckin' pockets right now!" he demanded.

Everybody watched Sam lower his head, take out everything he had in his pockets, and hand it to Tone.

"Yo, Maine, wash this nigga up," Tone told his best friend, whom he'd known since childhood. Immediately Maine covered his eyes as he busted the bottle of Grey Goose over Sam's head, dropping him instantly. Once the goons saw Sam's body hit the floor, they were all over him like vultures, kicking and stomping his face into the concrete.

"Mu'fucka must've thought shit was a game," Tone said out loud, stuffing the three hundred dollars that he just took from Sam into his pocket.

"How much that nigga was short?" Maine asked as him and Tone stood over on the side, and the goons continued to destroy what was left of Sam.

"Seven thousand."

Just then Tone noticed an unmarked car pull up to the scene, and seconds later out hopped a dark-skinned man with salt-and-pepper hair. From his muscular frame, you could tell that he still worked out often. Around his neck hung a shiny gold badge, and behind him was two uniformed cops.

When the goons spotted him, they immediately stopped the beating they was putting on Sam.

"Please don't stop 'cause I'm here." Detective Abraham smirked. "Fuck is going on out here?" He looked over at Tone.

"Mu'fucka owe, so he had to pay," Tone said nonchalantly.

Detective Abraham smoothly walked over to Maine, reaching inside his waistband and removing a .380 with a silencer on the muzzle. "Mu'fucka had to pay, huh?" As he stood over Sam's body, he fired three shots into his face. "What I told you about playing with mu'fuckas?" Detective Abraham growled. He slapped Tone in the back of his head. "I fuckin' taught you better than that."

"My bad, Pops," Tone said as he took the gun from his father's hand and passed it back to Maine.

"It's always your bad," Detective Abraham huffed as he walked back to his unmarked car followed by the two uniformed officers. "Be at my house first thing in the morning," he yelled over his shoulder as he slid back in his car and pulled off.

"Man, ya pops don't play," Maine said as he slid in the driver's seat of his all-black Audi.

"You know he just wants us to be the best we can be," Tone replied as he slid in the passenger seat. "He been telling me all week about this big plan he got for us. Finally, he suppose to spill the beans tomorrow."

"Well, whatever it is, you know it's a lot of paper involved," Maine said, knowing how much Detective Abraham loved money.

Maine pulled up in front of Tone's crib and threw his car in park. "Want me to come scoop you up tomorrow?"

"Nah. Just meet me at my pop's crib at like ten." Tone gave Maine a pound and slid out the passenger seat.

As soon as Tone stepped foot in the house, he saw his high-school sweetheart Mya in front of the TV doing her daily exercise with her Nintendo Wii. As soon as she spotted Tone, she quickly paused her game and headed over toward her man. Tone smiled as he watched his sexy-ass woman strut toward him wearing nothing but green boy shorts and matching bra. Mya favored the actress Vivica Fox but had a little more ass.

"Hey, baby," she said with a smile as she slid in Tone's arms.

Tone kissed Mya on the lips and playfully pushed her off of him. "Get outta here. You all sweaty and shit."

"Shut up. You know you love my sweat." She smiled as she walked over to the TV and continued her work-out.

After Tone helped himself to three shots of Grey Goose, he said,"How was your day?"

"It was okay. Had to stop these two bitches from fighting in the salon today. Other than that, it was a regular boring day," Mya told him as she jogged in place in front of the TV.

"I remember when you was begging me to get you your own salon, and now it's like you can't stand it." Tone laughed. "Women don't never know what they want."

"I love my salon. I just don't like all the people that come up there sometimes." Mya cut the TV off and headed to the bathroom so she could hop in the shower.

Tone headed over to the entertainment system and blasted Jay-Z's song, "Empire State of Mind." He sang along with Hov as he removed his .40-caliber from his waistband and sat it on the counter.

After he helped himself to another shot, he reached into his pocket and pulled out a ring box. He opened it and examined the diamond closely. He had been waiting for the perfect time to pop the question and thought tonight was the night.

"Hey," Mya said, appearing outta nowhere. "What you over there doing?" She was strolling through the house butt naked like she always did after her night shower.

"Minding my business." Tone smiled as he held the box behind his back.

Mya walked over to the entertainment system and turned the music down. "Why you always gotta have your music so damn loud?" When she turned around, her mouth hung wide open in shock.

Tone was on his knees and holding open the box with the ring. "Baby, will you marry me?"

"Yes!" Mya said loudly as she snatched the ring and put it on her finger.

Tone just smiled. He loved seeing Mya happy, but he had never seen her this happy. "Well . . . do you like it?"

Mya didn't answer. Instead, she walked over to Tone, unbuckled his belt, removed his dick, and slid down to her knees.

"Awww shit!" Tone moaned as he watched his fiancée work her magic.

Mya sucked and jerked on Tone's dick until he finally released in her mouth.

"Damn, baby," he said, breathing heavily. "Thanks."

"What you thanking me for? I'm just now getting started." Mya grabbed Tone's wrist and led him into the bedroom.

The next morning Tone woke up to his cell phone ringing. "Hello," he answered in a drowsy voice.

"Get ya ass over here," his father growled into the receiver.

Tone peeked over at the digital clock on the nightstand. "It's seven o'clock. You said to be there at ten."

"Be here in twenty minutes," Detective Abraham said, ending the conversation.

"Who was that, baby?" Mya asked, her eyes still closed.

"My father." Tone sat up to start getting dressed.

"Damn!" Mya whined. "You gotta go meet him right now?"

"Yeah. But I won't be gone too long, I promise."

After brushing his teeth, Tone stuck his .40-cal in his waistband and headed out the door.

Tone walked up to his father's front door and banged on it with an attitude. He hated getting up early. His father answered the door with a smile on his face.

"What the fuck is so important that I had to get outta my warm bed so early in the morning?" Tone asked, clearly upset.

Detective Abraham kept his smile up. "The early bird always gets the worm."

"Ain't no birds up this early." Tone headed inside and sat at the kitchen table.

"You wanna make some money or not?" Detective Abraham asked as he poured himself a drink.

"What you got up your sleeve now?" Tone asked, knowing his pops was always up to something.

"This what I got up my sleeve." Detective Abraham slid a folder toward his son.

Tone opened up the folder and saw a picture of an old Spanish-looking man. "Fuck is this?"

"His name is Santiago." Detective Abraham paused before adding, "He lives in L.A. now, but he's from Mexico. He's one of the biggest cocaine distributors in the world."

"So what you need me to do? Kill him?"

"Impossible," Detective Abraham said quickly. "We want to do business with him."

"So what's the big deal?" Tone asked, confused.

"The big deal is, he don't fuck with black people," Detective Abraham said with an angry look on his face. He hated racists, even though he was a racist himself.

"So where do I come in at in all of this?"

"Here's where you come in at." Detective Abraham slid his son another folder.

Tone opened the folder and saw a picture of a beautiful woman inside. "Who this?"

"That's Santiago's daughter, Serena."

"What does she have to do with anything?" Tone didn't like whatever his father was up to.

"She's in town for two weeks on vacation. She's staying at the New Yorker Hotel on Thirty-Fourth Street."

"And?"

"And you got two weeks to get in her head and convince her that you love her. Then once you get in good enough, you can get her to convince her father to do business with us." Detective Abraham smiled like he had everything all figured out.

"I don't know about this one, Pops," Tone said in deep thought.

"What's not to know? You wanna make some big money, right?"

"Yeah, but—"

"But nothing. It's a perfect plan."

"I ain't gon' be able to stay out the house for two weeks. Mya would kill me. Plus, we just got engaged last night."

"Fuck Mya! With the type of money you gonna be making, you can buy two more Myas." Detective Abraham chuckled, but he was dead serious.

But Tone didn't appreciate his father's remark about Mya. "Must you talk foolish all the time?"

"You know I was joking with you," Detective Abraham said, trying to downplay his comment. "All I'm saying is, you know Mya is a ride-or-die chick, so just explain to her what it is you gonna be doing, and you'll be fine."

"It ain't that easy, Pops. Mya is super jealous. I can't just say, 'Hey, baby, I'ma be fucking another bitch for two weeks,' and think she gonna be cool with that."

"Stop bitching and man up." Detective Abraham downed his drink in one gulp, only to refill his glass back up to the top. "You wanna make this money or what?"

"How much paper you think we can make if I can make this chick think I'm in love with her?"

"Millions!" Detective Abraham's eyes lit up just thinking about that amount of money. He didn't know how, but he had to make his son see what he saw, and he wasn't going to stop until he accomplished that mission.

"Damn! Two weeks is a short amount of time to make a bitch fall in love," Tone said out loud as he helped himself to a drink.

"I thought you was a pimp," Detective Abraham joked. "My name is John Abraham, and your name is Anthony Abraham. You know what that means?"

Tone smiled. "What?"

"That means you can do anything you put your mind to . . . trust me."

Detective Abraham heard somebody knocking at his front door. "Who is it?" he yelled, walking over to the door. He smiled when he saw Maine standing on the other side of the door. "Come on in."

"Y'all in here having a secret meeting without me?" Maine jokingly asked.

"Nah. Just going over a few things with this knucklehead over there." Detective Abraham motioned his head toward his son. "Speaking of knuckleheads . . . what was all that about last night?"

"That clown, Sam, owed us some bread, so we had to beat it outta him."

Maine loved putting in work and would do it for free, so getting paid for it was just a bonus.

"Nigga said some clown named Gruff robbed him, and some bitch named Maxine helped him," Tone told him.

"Who Gruff? From Brooklyn?" Detective Abraham asked, his voice rising a bit.

"Yeah, I think so," Tone answered. "Why? You know him?"

"I can't stand that muthafucka," Detective Abraham fumed. "Before I became a detective, I had many run-ins with that clown. Even whipped his ass once, me and my partner in an alley." He shook his head. "He ain't nothing but a trigger-happy nigga, in it for a street rep. He don't even care about the money."

"So what's up with him now?" Maine asked.

"Last I heard, he was on the run for some attempted murder charge," Detective Abraham said.

"What about the Maxine bitch?" Tone asked.

Detective Abraham shrugged his shoulders. "Never heard of her. She must be a new jack."

"Well, we ain't gotta worry about shit 'cause I'm gonna hunt that Gruff nigga down personally." Maine smirked.

"Let me just warn you," Detective Abraham said seriously as he placed his gaze on Maine, "that nigga Gruff gets busy."

"Good. 'Cause I get busy too," Maine said, a smirk still on his face.

"Fuck that clown Gruff," Detective Abraham said, waving him off. "I'ma need you focused 'cause you gonna be running shit for a while."

"Word?" Maine asked excitedly. "Why? What's up?"

"I put ya man Tone here on a mission that's going to last for a few weeks, so until then, you the man. Now both of y'all get the fuck outta here and make me proud," he said, dismissing the two.

Tone stepped out of his father's house not knowing how to feel. He wanted to make the money, but on the other hand, he didn't want Mya to be mad at him, or this job to ruin his healthy relationship. He knew Mya wasn't going to go for that shit, no matter how much money was involved.

"What's good? You a'ight?" Maine asked, sensing something was wrong.

"I'm good," Tone lied.

"What's good? You wanna run downtown with me? I'm supposed to be looking at this new car."

"Nah. I gotta head downtown to the New Yorker Hotel." Tone slid in his Benz and disappeared from his father's driveway.

Chapter 2

Tone pulled up in front of the New Yorker Hotel and let his engine die. "Fuck!" he said out loud as he grabbed the folder and took out the woman's picture to examine it. He tossed the picture back in the folder and leaned his head back against the headrest and waited patiently for his prey to either come in or exit the hotel.

Five hours later he saw the woman exit the hotel. "Damn!" He thought she was much prettier in person. The woman resembled the singer Keri Hilson, except for her hair that came down to the middle of her back. Her tall black boots made her calves and legs look toned and sexy. Just from looking at her, Tone could tell that she was stuck-up and used to the finer things in life.

He quickly made the engine of his Benz come to life with one turn of his key when his mark hopped in a yellow cab. He pulled out of his parking spot and followed the cab. After a short drive, the cab stopped at Forty-Second Street. Tone continued to follow the woman and watched her walk into Applebee's. He quickly pulled off and found a parking garage around the corner, where he parked his car, and headed over to Applebee's.

He walked inside the restaurant and saw his mark sitting over in a booth by the window looking through the menu.

"Just one?" the waitress politely asked him.

"Yeah." Tone followed the waitress over to a booth on the other side of the restaurant. "Excuse me, but is it possible for me to sit over there with that woman?" he asked.

"Well, sir, that's up to her," the waitress said, a confused look on her face.

"A'ight." Tone walked over and slid in the opposite side of the booth his mark was sitting at.

Serena sat in the booth over in the corner looking over her menu. She was starving and ready to eat. So far she'd been enjoying her vacation in New York. Her father always made sure she had the best of everything, and this time was no different. Once she decided what she wanted to eat, she looked up for the waitress. That's when she saw a handsome man heading over in her direction. He favored the singer Trey Songz but was a little rough around the edges. Serena watched as the man slid in her booth and sat opposite her.

"Can I help you?" she asked in a snotty tone.

"Oh, what's up?" Tone asked as he picked up the menu and began looking inside.

"Umm, can I help you?" Serena said, raising an eyebrow. "I mean, this is my table."

"I'm just tryin'a get something to eat and didn't wanna eat by myself." Tone paused. "And I saw a beautiful lady over here eating alone, so I thought, why not eat together?" He shrugged his shoulders.

Serena rolled her eyes. "How you know I wasn't waiting for someone?"

"Are you waiting for somebody?"

"That ain't the point," she said with a smile.

Tone returned her smile. "Nah, but for real, I had to come over here and talk to you. I've yet to see a woman as beautiful as you in my life. You must be from out of town, 'cause ain't no chicks out here that look like you."

"Yeah, I am from out of town, but beauty is only skin deep," Serena said in her West Coast accent.

The waitress walked up to the table, interrupting the conversation. "Are y'all ready to order?"

"Yes, ma'am," Tone said politely. "Can I have a steak, some French fries, and some rice, please?" he said as he handed the waitress back the menu.

The waitress looked at Serena. "And you, ma'am?"

"Yes, can I have some chicken fingers and some fries, please?"

"And to drink?"

Before Serena could say a word, Tone quickly replied, "Two Long Island ice teas please."

"Coming right up." The waitress smiled as she turned and disappeared through the double doors.

The two ate and talked for about an hour. As they sipped on their third Long Island ice tea, Tone asked, "So how long you in town for?" though he already knew the answer.

"Two weeks."

"Damn! So I don't got much time then?"

"Much time for what?" she asked suspiciously.

"To try and convince you to stay," Tone said with a smile.

Serena chuckled. "I like New York, but that doesn't mean I wanna live here."

"I can dig it." Tone smiled. "So what you doing later on?"

"Nothing. Probably just gonna sit in my room and watch movies all night."

"Fuck that!" Tone said, canceling her movie night. "I'm taking you out tonight. I'm not gonna let you spend your two weeks here just sitting up in a room."

Serena liked the way Tone was taking control, and the way he carried himself. "What did you have in mind?"

"Just be ready around eight o'clock," Tone said with a smile as him and Serena got up and exited the restaurant.

"Yo, what you doing?" Tone asked when he saw Serena trying to flag down a cab.

"Trying to get a cab," she said innocently.

"Don't disrespect me like that." Tone smiled. "Wait right there."

Five minutes later Tone pulled up to the corner in his Benz. Once Serena got in, he quickly pulled off.

Maine double-parked his Denali in front of the projects. Now that he was in charge while Tone was on that other mission, he planned on letting it be known that he was moving up in the empire and wasn't taking no shit. He walked up to a building, where about five local guys stood in front. "What's good? How's it looking out here?" Maine asked as he gave each man dap.

"Slow motion," a skinny cat named Calvin answered.

"Yo, any of y'all seen Gruff out here lately?" Maine asked.

"I saw that cat the other day," Calvin said, searching his memory.

"Word? You know where I can catch up with him at?"

"Nah. You know Gruff moves like the wind. It's hard to catch him in one spot," Calvin reminded him. "Why? Something up?"

"Nah, we cool. I just got something I need to give him," Maine said as he headed in the building.

After waiting a few minutes for the elevator, Maine decided to take the stairs to the fifth floor. He walked down the hall until he found the door he was looking for. He knocked and waited for a reply. He heard somebody fiddling with the locks. A man with a messed-up Afro opened the door and stepped to the side for Maine to enter.

"Damn, nigga! Why it always smell like ass when I come up in here?" Maine huffed, his nose wrinkled up.

"Fuck outta here! I ain't smell shit until you got here," Afro capped back.

"Man, just gimme what you got for me, so I can get up outta here." Maine covered his mouth and nose with his shirt as he watched Afro head toward the back.

Afro returned with a book bag. "Take this and get the fuck out! Coming up in here, funking my shit all up with that cheap-ass cologne you got on." He escorted Maine to the door. Every time him and Maine got together the two would go at it.

"Fuck outta here!" Maine said, walking out the apartment. "Nigga, you smell like a dead body," he yelled over his shoulder and disappeared through the staircase door.

Maine slid back behind the wheel of his Denali when he heard his cell phone ringing. Instantly he recognized the number. "What's good?"

"Got a little problem I need you to solve for me," Detective Abraham told him.

"E-mail me the nigga résumé."

A minute later Maine checked the e-mail on his phone, and an address and profile picture came up of his target. He quickly punched the address in his navigational system and headed toward the destination.

Detective Abraham sat in an all-black van along with three of his crooked partners. For about two weeks, they had been scoping out Big Mike's dope house. Detective Abraham was tired of watching him get rich. He took a deep drag from his Newport. "Damn! This nigga spot is really clicking."

Maxwell, one of Abraham's crooked partners, said, "Yeah, he going to have to come up off this spot."

"Y'all muthafuckas ready?" Detective Abraham asked as he loaded his MAC-11.

All three of his partners nodded their heads yes.

"Let's do it."

Detective Abraham slid out the van and ran up toward the back door. He silently counted to three and watched Maxwell kick the back door open.

"Police! Nobody move!" Detective Abraham yelled as he stormed inside.

Big Mike tried to grab the AK-47 that sat next to him, but he quickly put the assault rifle back down when he realized they had the drop on him.

"Don't fucking move!" Detective Abraham said, his MAC-11 trained on the drug dealer.

"Fuck y'all pigs want?" Big Mike asked with an attitude. "Y'all want money, or y'all came to lock me up this time?"

"Depends." Detective Abraham smiled. "How much money you got up in here?"

"About fifty thousand. Why?"

"Hand that over," Detective Abraham said quickly.

"It's over there in the safe," Big Mike said.

Just then somebody knocked on Big Mike's door.

"That's just one of my customers," he said nonchalantly.

Maxwell looked over and saw the table covered with bundled-up dope. He grabbed a few bundles and walked to the door and served the fiend.

Detective Abraham smiled as he dialed his son's number.

On the fifth ring, Tone finally answered. "What up?"

"I need you to send me a few workers over here," Detective Abraham told him. "Got us a new spot."

"I got you. Just e-mail me the address," Tone said as he ended the call.

Once Detective Abraham hung up the phone, he quickly e-mailed Tone the info he needed.

"Y'all already got the money. Now what?" Big Mike said.

"Now you say good night."

Detective Abraham smiled as he raised his MAC-11 and pulled the trigger. The rest of the crew watched Big Mike's body jerk back and forth as the bullets ripped through him.

"Clean this mess up. Call me and let me know when the workers get here." Detective Abraham walked out the dope house like nothing never happened. This was just the beginning of his big plan. Plus, who was going to stop him? He was the police.

"A'ight," Tone said to his workers, "I need y'all over there as soon as possible. One."

As soon as he hung up the phone, Mya was all over him. "Where you going, looking all nice?"

"Looking all nice?" Tone echoed. "I got on regular clothes."

"I thought you was taking me out tonight," Mya whined. She had been waiting all day for Tone to come home so they could go out, like he had promised.

"I was, but I gotta do something for my pops tonight."

"But you promised me. Can't you do whatever it is you gotta do for him tomorrow?"

"Nah, it's gotta be done tonight. Sorry." Tone kissed Mya on her forehead. "But, I promise you, I won't be out too late." Then he stuck his .40-cal in his waistband and headed out the door.

Maine pulled up in front of the building his GPS led him to. He quickly pulled out his .380 and screwed on the silencer before exiting his whip. He walked in the building and took the stairs to the third floor. When he reached the apartment he was looking for, he flung his hood over his head as he knocked on the door. Once he saw somebody looking through the peephole, he quickly raised his gun up to it and pulled the trigger once. After Maine heard the body drop, he shot off the doorknob. Then he busted up in the apartment and shot the body that lay on the floor two more times before shutting the door behind him.

As Maine slowly eased his way through the apartment, he could hear soft R&B music coming from the back room. Holding his gun in a two-handed grip as he approached the back room, he quickly busted up in the room and saw a woman breast-feeding an infant. He raised his gun and sent a bullet through her skull. The woman collapsed straight back on the bed, and the baby rolled out of her arms onto the floor, screaming at the top of its lungs.

Maine checked the rest of the apartment to make sure there was nobody else inside. Then he disappeared out the front door.

Maine pulled up in front of his crib and let the engine die as he stepped out the car. As soon as he walked in the door, he saw his girlfriend Monique halfway dressed, and two of her girlfriends sitting on the couch.

"Fuck you going?" he asked.

"Out," Monique replied. "You think I'm supposed to be stuck up in this house all muthafuckin' day while you just out doing whatever? I don't think so."

"I know that's right," one of her girlfriends cooed.

"I'm out getting money," Maine said, nodding down to the blood on his shoes. "And you out running the streets."

"I can't go out every now and then with my girls? Why I always gotta be 'running the streets'? You must be out doing dirt. That's probably why you never want me to go nowhere."

"You know what? Just get your shit and get the fuck out!"

Monique smiled, her hands on her hips. "You kicking me out?"

"Either get out, or get put out," Maine said in an even tone.

Monique saw the look in Maine's eyes and knew he wasn't bullshitting.

"Fuck you, nigga!"

Monique huffed as she grabbed a few things from out the back room. "Bitch-ass nigga! I was doing you a favor staying here. Talking 'bout get out or get put out—I wish you would put your muthafuckin' hands on me!"

"You see, if I had a white bitch, I wouldn't have to go through this kinda shit," Maine spat. He knew she hated to see a white woman with a black man.

"Nigga, fuck you and your white bitch! I wish I would catch you with a white bitch. I'll beat you and that bitch's ass!"

"Just get out!" Maine smirked. "And hurry the fuck up!"

"Get a good look 'cause you ain't gon' never see me or this ass again," Monique said as her and her friends left, leaving the front door wide open.

Maine closed the door and flopped down on the couch. After a long day, all he wanted to do was have a drink, get some head, and watch a movie until he fell asleep, but instead he had to come home to chaos and foolishness.

Chapter 3

Tone pulled up in front of the New Yorker Hotel and saw Serena standing out front looking super sexy. He tapped the horn twice and watched as Serena strutted toward the Benz and slid in the passenger seat.

She kissed Tone on the cheek. "I thought you was tryin'a stand me up."

"Damn! A nigga can't even be five minutes late." Tone smiled as he pulled out into traffic.

"So where we going?"

"To go eat," Tone answered quickly.

Thirty minutes later Tone pulled up to a nice soul food restaurant. "You like soul food?"

"I love soul food," Serena answered with her glossed-up lips. "I'm glad you brought me here."

"Why? What's up? You wanna go somewhere else?"

"Nah, I just don't like being around a lot of bushy people. I just like eating around down-to-earth people," she tried to explain.

"I feel you." Tone smiled.

Serena liked that the clientele at this soul food restaurant was mixed, with white, black, and Spanish customers. That meant that the food was tasty, and appealing to everybody.

Once the two were seated, Serena popped the million-dollar question. "So what do you do for a living?"

Tone smiled. "You want me to lie or tell the truth?"

"Both," Serena said, matching his smile.

"Okay, I'm the local cable man, and I do electrician on the side."

"Okay, now the truth," Serena said, shaking her head and smiling.

Tone paused before he answered, "I control a big drug empire," looking at Serena for her reaction.

"Fuck it! We all gotta do what we gotta do," she said seriously.

Her response caught Tone off guard. "So you cool with that?"

"Yeah, my uncle and a few of his peoples used to fuck around in the drug game, and half of my family use drugs. So I'm no stranger to that type of stuff."

"You ever had a boyfriend that was into that life-style?"

"Not yet. Why you ask?"

"'Cause, as you can see, I'm really feeling you. Everything about you. I've yet to meet a woman who I can talk to on some regular shit, feel me?"

"I feel you, but this ain't gonna work."

"What you mean? Why not?"

"Because we live in two different cities. And you have a life, and so do I."

"What if I want you in my life?" Tone pressed.

"How are you so sure? You don't know me like that."

"I want to get to know you," Tone said, looking Serena in her eyes. "I don't care if I have to come out to L.A. once a month so we can be together. Whatever I have to do, I'ma do it."

Serena smirked. "I hear you talking."

"I let my actions do my talking," Tone countered.

The two ate their food and sat and talked for about forty-five minutes in the restaurant before leaving. As they walked back to the car, Tone felt his phone vibrating. He looked at the caller ID and saw that it was Mya.

He quickly put his phone on silent as he put it back in the case.

"So what you got planned for the rest of the night?" Tone asked as he slid in the driver's seat.

"Go back to my room and get some rest."

"You want some company?"

"That would be nice." Serena smiled. "But that don't mean you getting none of this good pussy."

Tone smirked. "I just wanna spend as much time with you as I can before you leave," he said as he pulled into traffic.

As the two drove chitchatting, a crackhead flagged the Benz down like his life depended on it.

"Fuck!" Tone huffed as he quickly pulled over to the side of the road and rolled his window down.

Serena was about to say something but decided to just keep quiet.

The crackhead ran up to the driver's window all out of breath. "Tone, wassup, man? I thought that was you," he said, trying to fix the collar on his shirt.

"Fuck you doing out here, Malcolm?" Tone asked, not looking the fiend directly in his eyes.

"Just out tryin'a get some fresh air." Malcolm wiped the slime from the corners of his mouth. "You got a few dollars you can spare so I can go get me something to eat?"

Tone pulled five twenties from his knot and handed them to Malcolm. "Swing by my house tomorrow night so we can get you straightened up."

"Okay, I got you." Malcolm hurried off across the street.

Tone pulled off, a frown on his face.

"You okay?" Serena asked.

"Yeah, I'm fine," he huffed. "It just bothers me to see him all fucked up like that."

"He a close friend of yours?"

"Nah, that's my brother."

"Oh, I'm sorry to hear that."

"It's all good," Tone said as he pulled up in front of the New Yorker Hotel.

"You still coming up?" Serena asked.

"Nah, I'm about to go back and try to find my brother before he gets himself killed," Tone said, a sad look on his face.

"Okay. You know where I'm at if you need me." Serena kissed Tone on his cheek and headed inside the hotel.

As soon as she disappeared inside the hotel, Tone pulled out his cell phone and dialed his pops' number.

"What you want?" Detective Abraham grumbled into the receiver.

"I just saw Malcolm out here."

"Fuck you telling me for?"

"Maybe because that's your son."

"That muthafucka ain't my son!"

"Malcolm out here looking real bad, Pops. He needs our help."

"Fuck Malcolm! I done helped that boy as much as I can. Once a muthafucka steal out my house, he ain't considered family no more. He lucky I didn't kill his ass!"

"He's still your son, no matter what."

"The only son I got is you, and if you start getting high, then fuck you too!" Detective Abraham hung up in Tone's ear.

"Ignorant muthafucka!"

As soon as Tone stepped foot in the crib, he found Mya sitting in the living room waiting for him, a scarf on her head and her arms folded. "So we not answering phones now?"

"Not tonight, baby, please," Tone said as he walked in the kitchen.

Mya quickly shot to her feet. "Fuck you mean, not tonight? You gon' tell me something."

"I was out and ran into Malcolm," Tone said, pouring himself some orange juice.

Mya knew the deal about his brother's bad crack problem and felt bad about it. "How is he?" she said, her whole tone changing.

"He look bad. I just hate to see him all fucked up and shit. No matter what I do to try and help, it seems like nothing works."

"He ain't gonna get that monkey off his back until he's ready to," Mya said, rubbing her man's back. "Trust me, only he'll know when enough is enough."

"You right."

After Tone went to the back, took a shower, and got in the bed, Mya hopped on his dick and rode it like there was no tomorrow, until the two both came then fell fast asleep in each other's arms.

Chapter 4

"So what I been missing?" Tone sipped on some vodka and orange juice. He looked around the warehouse and saw about ten to twelve soldiers just sitting around, telling lies and war stories.

"You ain't really been missing shit." Maine, who was drinking his vodka straight, downed his drink. "Your pops done busted mad drug dealers and took over their spots."

"Word?"

"Yeah. So I put a few soldiers in each spot." Maine picked up the new machine gun he had just purchased and started tinkering with it. "But what's good with you and that honey?"

"She cool." Tone sipped his drink. "I think I can pull it off."

"Well, shit. At least you gon' get some pussy out of the deal." Maine smiled. "I heard she fine too."

Tone smiled. "Yeah, she good, money."

"Yeah, I bet."

Just then Maine's cell phone started ringing. He answered, "Yeah, who this?"

"Yo, this Li'l Man. That nigga Gruff out here in the projects right now. Get down here fast 'cause I think he about to leave."

"Be there in a minute." Maine hung up the phone, grabbed his new machine gun, and headed toward the door.

"Yo," Tone called out, "where you going?"

"Just got the drop on that clown Gruff. I'll be back in a second," he said as he disappeared out the door.

Tone shook his head. He smiled when he saw Serena's name flashing across the screen of his cell phone. "What's good, ma?" he answered.

"You tell me," she capped back. "I was just calling to see what was up for tonight."

"I mean, what you wanna do? You know I'm down for whatever," Tone told her.

"I think I wanna go out tonight, so put on your dancing shoes and come pick me up tonight."

"Say no more. I got you. I'll see you in about two hours."

"A'ight, I'll be waiting."

Maine pulled up to the projects and double-parked his car on the ave and hopped out with his hoodie on, one hand tucked in his pocket. He wasn't there to play no games, and couldn't wait to teach this street punk they called Gruff a lesson he would never forget. Immediately he walked straight up to Li'l Man. "What's good? Gruff still out here?"

"You just missed him," Li'l Man said with a smirk on his face.

"Something funny?"

"Nah, I'm just saying . . . what you looking for Gruff for? That nigga looked like he just killed ten people."

Maine gave Li'l Man a comical look. He thought he sounded like a bitch. "So what? You his cheerleader now?"

"Nah, I'm just saying, I did time with him back in the day, and he a cool-ass nigga."

"Let me ask you a question"—Maine step
Li'l Man's face—"Gruff putting money in ya
pocket?"

"Nah, it's not even—"

Maine quickly stole on the li'l nigga, knocking him
out with one punch. "Bum-ass nigga," he mumbled as
he stepped over Li'l Man's body and hopped back in his
whip. "I'm tired of playing with these niggas," he said
to nobody in particular as he headed over to the crib of
one of Tone's workers to go pick up some paper that he
owed.

"You not leaving out this house another night until
you tell me what's going on," Mya said, standing in
front of the door so Tone couldn't leave.

"What is you talking about?" Tone huffed. He knew
sooner or later this moment was going to come. "Move
out the way."

"Fuck you!" Mya spat, not budging. "You done been
out to the wee hours in the morning for the past three
days, you gon' tell me something."

"Okay, okay. I been kicking it with this chick for the
last three days."

Mya smirked as she threw her hair in a raggedy ponytail. "You been doing what?" She charged him, swinging.

Tone grabbed Mya's arms and wrestled her down to
the floor and sat on top of her. "Chill."

"All the shit we done been through, and you out with
another bitch?" Mya growled, struggling to get up off
the floor.

"Listen!" Tone yelled in her face. "I have to spend
time with her. Her father is a big-time cat, and we just
need her to feel comfortable with me so she can plug
me in, that's all."

"Who the fuck is 'we'?"

"My pops."

"He always getting you in some shit. Why the fuck can't you ever tell him no?" Mya asked, tears escaping from her eyes. She hated Tone's father, who was always influencing him to do some dumb shit. If it wasn't one thing, it was another.

"Baby, this shit is only gonna take two weeks, I promise you."

"What about us?"

"What you mean?" Tone asked, confused.

"We just got engaged the other day. How you just gonna be fuckin' with another woman? Did you even take the time out to think about how I would feel?" Mya didn't wait for him to reply before she added, "If I was out for two weeks with another man, how the fuck would you feel?"

"Listen, I gotta do what I gotta do, point-blank. This is too much money to pass up on."

"Oh, so now you a prostitute? 'Cause a prostitute will do anything for money, so I guess you a prostitute."

Tone sighed loudly as he got up off Mya and headed for the door.

"You walk out that door, you ain't gotta worry about coming back," Mya said, hoping to stop her fiancé from leaving, but Tone just walked straight out the door.

"Fuck you!" she spat as she tossed the ring he had just given her a few nights before at the back of his head. "Take that piece a shit with you, you punk-ass bitch!" she yelled and slammed the door.

Tone hopped in his all-black Range Rover and pulled out the driveway. He couldn't believe how Mya was acting. As much as they had been through, he couldn't understand why she couldn't just hold it down for two weeks. She knew she was the one he wanted to marry, so what was the big deal?

Bitches always care more about love than money. But if a nigga didn't have shit and still lived with his mother, then we wouldn't've even had a relationship to start with. Fuck that! Ain't no bitch 'bout to fuck up my money. He popped in 50 Cent's new CD. *Once I get all this money, she'll love me again in two weeks,* he thought to himself as he hit the highway, headed downtown to pick Serena up.

Maine stood in the lobby waiting for the elevator. "This shit need to hurry up," he said. In a rush to get to the strip club, he was ready to just chill for the rest of the night, get drunk, and see some freaks. He stepped in the elevator and pressed the floor he was headed to repeatedly. Once the elevator reached his floor, he stepped off and found himself looking down the barrels of two 9 mm's.

"I heard you was looking for me," Gruff said with a smile. "I would've ran down on you sooner, but I didn't even know what you looked like until earlier."

Meanwhile, Gruff's partner in crime, Maxine, stripped Maine of his .380 with the silencer on it.

Maine peeped that both stickup kids wore all-black. Gruff wore a hoodie that right there told him that he didn't play, because he didn't even bother to hide his face.

"Nigga, get ya bitch ass over here!" Maxine growled. She grabbed Maine by the collar of his shirt and pushed him in front of the door he was looking for. "Knock, muthafucka!"

Maine wanted to turn around and knock the little bitch with the tough-guy talk the fuck out, but he knew at that moment he couldn't. So he did as he was told and knocked on the door.

Immediately, Rodney opened the door. "Damn, nigga! What the fuck took you so damn long?"

Gruff quickly tossed one of his 9s in Rodney's face. "Back up, playboy!" he said, busting his way up in the apartment and shoving Rodney to the floor. He quickly duct taped Rodney's hands.

Gruff then turned his attention on Maine. "Fuck you out here looking for me for?"

"You took something that belonged to me from someone else," Maine answered.

"That sound like ya man's problem." Gruff smiled. "Fuck that gotta do with me and you?"

"I'm the enforcer," Maine answered simply.

"So you just doing your job, right?"

"Yeah"

"Me too." Gruff nodded at Maxine, who hit Maine upside his head with her .357.

Maine turned and tried to charge the bitch, but Gruff quickly put a bullet in his leg, dropping him instantly.

"Yo, fam, where you keep that money at?" Gruff asked, looking at Rodney.

"In the kitchen under the sink," he answered quickly, not wanting to get shot like Maine.

Maxine quickly walked over to the kitchen and retrieved the money.

"Listen, Maine," Gruff said, squatting so Maine could hear him clearly, "don't take this personal, but I'm just doing my job. Either respect it or check it!" Then him and Maxine headed for the door.

Before Maxine exited the apartment, she walked over and kicked Maine in his face.

Maine lay on the floor holding his bloody leg. He was mad that he had got caught slipping, but he smiled because he was still alive. He knew that the two stickup kids would definitely see him again. He struggled to his feet and leaned up against the wall for support and eased his way up out of the apartment.

"Yo, untie me," Rodney yelled at Maine's departing back, but Maine ignored him.

Detective Abraham sat on his couch watching a young sexy stripper entertain him. He hated strip clubs, 'cause there was always too many people around. He liked his shows private and in his house. That way, once the show was over, he could fuck the stripper right in his house instead of in some champagne room.

The young sexy stripper bent over and jiggled her titties in Abraham's face while he palmed her ass and whispered pervert shit in her ear. His whisper came to an end when he heard somebody banging on the door like the police.

"What the fuck?" Detective Abraham pushed the stripper out of his face and removed a .44 Magnum from under the couch cushion. He eased his way to the door. "Who the fuck is it?"

"Maine!"

"Fuck you want?" Detective Abraham quickly snatched open the door.

"Yo, I need your help," Maine said, helping himself inside, blood dripping everywhere.

Immediately Detective Abraham helped Maine to the kitchen and, with one swipe, knocked everything off the countertop and helped Maine get up there.

He looked over and saw the stripper fully dressed. "Fuck!" he said under his breath. He walked over to her and handed her a hundred-dollar bill. "Baby, I gotta take care of a li'l something, as you can see, but make sure you call me tomorrow."

The stripper kissed Detective Abraham on the cheek and promised she'd call him the next day then made her exit.

Detective Abraham quickly picked his house phone and called a crooked street doctor that had been in the family for years. After he hung up the phone, he said to Maine. "What the fuck happened to you?"

Maine looked over Detective Abraham and, through clenched teeth, said, "Gruff!"

The club was jumping when Tone and Serena stepped foot inside. Serena danced a little bit, while Tone just stood by the wall drinking some Alizé straight from the bottle, just enjoying the scene. Dancing was never really his thing.

Serena smiled. "Come and dance with me."

"Nah, chill. That's not even my flow." Tone threw his bottle up again.

"Pleasssssse?" Serena sang as she grabbed his hand and pulled him out to the dance floor.

As Tone headed toward the dance floor, he could feel the eyes of all the other hustlers on Serena. When they got to the dance floor, Serena placed her soft ass on his dick and began grinding and gyrating her hips to the beat like she was having sex. Tone grabbed Serena's waist with one hand and started grinding even harder into her as he turned up his bottle again. The two danced for four songs straight before Tone headed back over by the wall, where he continued to watch Serena enjoy herself.

Tone felt his cell phone vibrating on his hip. He removed it from its case and read the text message that his pops had sent him: SOMEBODY CROSSED MAINE UP AND HIT HIM WITH A JUMP SHOT GET HERE ASAP

Just as Tone was putting his phone back in its case, Serena walked up. "You enjoying yourself?" She took the Alizé bottle from Tone and took a deep swig.

"Something just came up, and we gotta go." Tone grabbed Serena's hand and led her out of the club.

Once outside, Serena asked, "You sure everything is okay?"

"My homie just got shot."

Just then Tone saw some big, dirty nigga named Big Phil. Tone always saw Big Phil around, but the two never spoke to each other. Big Phil was a nigga who talked big shit and liked to put on a show for the crowd. He was also known as being a disrespectful motherfucker. Immediately Tone saw Big Phil's eyes land on Serena.

Big Phil stopped dead in his tracks and shook his head. "Now that's what you call a ass," he said, craning his neck to get a better look at Serena's ass.

Tone stepped toward Big Phil. "Fuck you just say?" Tone wasn't mad about what Big Phil said, he was mad 'cause he felt that Big Phil was trying to disrespect him in front of a crowd.

"Fuck is you getting all hot for? I was just giving your joint a compliment," Big Phil said. "But if you wanna get ignorant, that ain't no problem either." He lifted his shirt and exposed the butt of his gun.

Immediately Serena jumped in front of Tone. "Let's go, baby. He ain't worth it. I'm not gonna let you go to jail over this loser," she said as she escorted him through the parking lot.

"Yeah, that's what I thought," Big Phil said loud enough so Tone and Serena could hear him. "You better listen to your bitch and get outta here before you get hurt."

Tone reached his whip and quickly grabbed his .40-cal from underneath the seat.

Before he could turn around, Serena was right in front of him. "Let it go, please," she pleaded. "It's not worth it."

Tone sighed loudly as he slid behind the wheel. Once Serena hopped in the passenger seat, he quickly pulled off. If Serena wasn't with him, he would've gone back and blown Big Phil's head off for trying to play him like that, but for the moment he had to suck it up and let it go. He knew he would definitely run into Big Phil again, and it would be more than words being exchanged.

Chapter 5

Tone pulled up in front of his father's house and threw the Range in park. He was still mad at Big Phil trying to stunt on him back there, all the things that he really wanted to do to the man running through his mind all at the same time.

"I'll be back in a second," he said to Serena as he slid out the Range. He walked up to his father's house and knocked lightly.

Detective Abraham snatched the door open, a frown on his face.

"What happen?" Tone asked as soon as he stepped in the kitchen and saw Maine laid up with his leg all wrapped up.

"Tough guy over here decided he wanted to go out and look for Gruff," Detective Abraham volunteered, shaking his head.

"He gon' have to answer for this," Maine said.

Detective Abraham told him, "The plan was for you to handle business while Tone was absent for a while, not start an unnecessary war."

"He already took money out of our pockets once." Maine placed his gaze on Detective Abraham. "And I'll be damned if I let it happen again."

"Take care of business first!" Detective Abraham yelled. "Once business is taken care of, I could care less what you do."

"I got shorty outside," Tone cut in. "Can I come holla at y'all tomorrow?"

"She outside right now?" Detective Abraham asked, a wicked smirk on his face.

"Yeah, she sitting in the car."

"Did you get the connect yet?"

"Stop being so thirsty." Tone waved his pops off. "I'ma get it."

Detective Abraham pointed a finger at his son. "Don't be falling in love with this bitch. Don't forget this is business."

"I got this, old man," Tone said, ending the conversation at that.

Tone slid back behind the wheel of the Range Rover. "I want you to spend a night with me," he said, looking at Serena for a response.

"Let's go."

"That was easy." Tone smiled as he pulled off, headed to his other condo out in Jersey.

Tone pulled into his parking spot and let the engine die.

"This is it," he said as the two entered the condo. "Make yourself at home."

Serena immediately kicked off her heels and let the thick carpet massage her feet. "This is a nice place you got here," she said looking around, impressed at how clean and nice-looking his crib was, especially for a single man.

Tone returned from the kitchen carrying two drinks in his hand.

"So was your friend okay?" Serena asked as they sat on the couch in front of the 70-inch flat-screen.

"Yeah, he fine. It was just a leg shot."

Tone took a deep sip from his drink. "So you had fun tonight?"

"I sure did." Serena smiled. "I appreciate you hanging out with me."

"Don't mention it. I just wish I had a little more than a week and a half to spend with you."

"Let's just worry about now. Nobody knows what lies ahead for the future," Serena said as she laid her head on Tone's shoulder.

The two sat up talking for hours, until Serena got up to stretch. "Is it okay if I take a shower before bed?" she asked.

"Sure." Tone pointed. "It's up the steps and the first door on your right."

He watched Serena's ass switch from side to side as she mounted the steps.

While Serena was upstairs handling her business, Tone walked over to the entertainment center and popped in a Mary J. Blige CD. He stood over by the bar area pouring himself another drink when he saw Serena coming down the steps wrapped in a towel.

Tone looked at Serena's meaty thighs. "Damn!"

"Boy, hush. You know I didn't bring a change of clothes with me." Serena walked up and took Tone's glass from his hand. She slowly sipped it.

As she sipped from the glass, Tone smoothly removed her towel. Immediately Serena slid in Tone's arms, and the two passionately kissed, his hands running freely all over her body.

He lifted Serena up and sat her on top of the counter, and she quickly spread her legs open. Tone dropped down and began eating her pussy. He stuck his fingers in Serena's sopping-wet pussy as he sucked on her clitoris like his future depended on it.

"You like that?" he asked. He grabbed his glass of wine, poured a little bit on her pussy, and quickly sucked it off.

Once Tone was finished, Serena hopped off the counter and slid down to her knees. She roughly pulled Tone's pants down and started sucking the shit out of his dick. Serena's head bobbed up and down a hundred miles an hour, both of her hands moving at the same speed, while she sucked and jerked his dick at the same time.

After five minutes of that, Tone quickly backed away as he turned Serena around and watched her bend over and placed her forearms on the counter. He slowly stuck the head inside her before fully entering her walls. Once he was fully in, he started fucking the shit out of her and talking shit at the same time.

"You love this dick?" he groaned, slapping her ass.

"Yes. This dick feel so good." Serena started throwing her ass back.

Tone continued dicking Serena down until he felt himself about to come. He quickly pulled out and came all over Serena's ass.

"Damn!" he huffed, collapsing right on the floor, breathing heavily. He didn't expect Serena's sex game to be as good as it was.

After he was done, he felt bad about what he had just done and what he was doing, but at the end of the day he had to do what he had to do. He told himself he was doing it for him and his family, hoping it would make him feel better, but it didn't.

Chapter 6

Three days later Tone pulled up in front of Maine's crib and left the engine running. He knocked on the door and patiently waited for a response.

A young thug answered the door. "Yeah?"

"Fuck out my way!" Tone snarled as he brushed past the young street punk. He reached the living room and saw Maine laid up on the couch. "What's good, my nigga?" Tone asked as he gave Maine a pound.

"Just laying low until my leg heal. What you getting into today?"

"Gotta finish picking up this money," Tone said. "Who the last person you saw so I can take it from there?"

"Ummm . . . that li'l nigga Rice." Maine suddenly remembered.

"A'ight, bet." Tone turned on his heels and headed for the door.

"Yo, hold up," Maine called out. "Ya pops said for you to take this nigga with you." He motioned his head at the young nigga who had opened the door.

"Who? This nigga right here?" Tone asked, his face crumpled up.

"Yup." Maine laughed.

"Yo, fam, what's ya name?"

"Young Mike."

"Come on, li'l nigga, let's go," Tone said with an attitude as he exited the apartment.

Once they got to the car Young Mike said, "I appreciate the opportunity."

"Just shut up and ride." Tone popped in a Young Jeezy mixtape and pulled off out into traffic.

Tone pulled over and let the engine die. "You strapped?"

"You already know," Young Mike said confidently as the two exited the vehicle. Young Mike followed Tone inside the building to an apartment all the way to the end of the hall.

Tone knocked on the door and waited for an answer. A short guy wearing a wifebeater answered the door.

"What's good?" Li'l Carlos stepped to the side so the two men could enter.

"You tell me," Tone said, posting up. "You got that for me?"

"Yeah, it's right here." Li'l Carlos grabbed the book bag from off the table and handed it to Tone.

"Nah. Give it to him," Tone said, nodding toward Young Mike, who took the book bag from Li'l Carlos and handed him the half-empty garbage bag he was carrying.

"I should be done with this in like two days," Li'l Carlos said, looking inside the garbage bag.

"You know what to do when you get low." Tone gave Li'l Carlos a pound, and him and Young Mike made their exit.

For the rest of the day Tone rode around with Young Mike taking care of business. After hours of talking to the young hustler, he found out that Young Mike wasn't that bad after all.

"I'm hungrier than a muthafucka," Young Mike said.

"This the last run for the night. We grab something to eat soon as we finish." Tone was about to say something else to Young Mike, when he saw a familiar face standing on the corner. He quickly pulled over. "Let's switch places," he said, and him and Young Mike switched seats.

"What's good?" Young Mike asked.

"Clown I got a problem with back there standing on the corner like shit is sweet," Tone said as he pulled out his .40-cal. "Pull this muthafucka back around and slow down when we hit the corner."

Young Mike made a quick U-turn and slowed down when he reached the corner, where Big Phil stood talking to a few of his workers. He had only planned on being there for about five minutes, but twenty minutes later he found himself on the corner laughing and poppin' shit.

"A'ight, slow down right here," Tone said. As soon as he saw Big Phil, he stuck his arm out the window and squeezed the trigger repeatedly.

POW! POW! POW! POW! POW!

The first shot hit Big Phil in his hip, causing him to spin around and hit the ground.

Big Phil quickly pulled out his Smith & Wesson and fired three shots into the back door.

Tone laid down three more people who stood on the corner, before he pulled his arm back inside the window. "Don't drive so fast." Tone wiped his prints off the gun then tossed it out the window.

Young Mike pulled up in front of his crib and slid out the driver's seat. "Holla at me tomorrow," he said as he gave Tone a pound.

"I got you." Tone walked around the car and slid back in the driver's seat.

***

Tone pulled up in his driveway and let the engine die, he slid out the whip, popped the trunk, grabbed the suitcase that rested inside, slammed the trunk shut, then headed in the house. Soon as he walked in the crib, he saw Serena standing over the stove wearing nothing but a wifebeater. His eyes quickly locked on Serena's phat, soft ass.

"Oooh!" Serena grabbed her heart. "You scared the shit outta me."

"My bad." Tone smiled as he watched Serena walk toward him. "How was your day?"

Serena slid in his arms for a hug. "It was cool. I just wish you wasn't gone all day, but I know you was out working, so it's all good."

After the two locked lips, Tone said, "Oh here," and handed Serena the suitcase. "I stopped by your room and grabbed all your shit, since you'll be staying here with me until you leave." He put on his puppy-dog face.

"Oh, shut up!" Serena said playfully as she headed back over toward the stove.

"What you cooking? That shit smell mad good."

"It's a surprise." Serena smiled. "Just know you're gonna love it."

"How long it's gon' take until it's done?"

Tone was really enjoying his time with Serena. The two had only known each other for a short time, but so far she seemed like the perfect woman.

"It should be ready in about twenty minutes." Serena slowly unbuckled Tone's belt and pulled his pants and boxers down. "Did he miss me today?" she asked, getting down to her knees.

Before Tone could reply, he was already moaning and panting as Serena sucked the shit out his dick. She moaned loudly while twisting and turning her hands and head at the same time until Tone came in her mouth.

Serena quickly walked over to the garbage and spat then went back to finishing up dinner.

Chapter 7

"You sure this gonna be a easy lick?" Maxine asked.

"Easier than taking candy from a baby." Gruff rubbed the head of his pit bull. "Ain't that right, Tiger," he said, talking to his dog. He had raised the dog since she was a puppy, and now the pit bull looked like a monster. Gruff wasn't into robbing and sticking people up for the money. Of course, the money was good, but he did it for the name and street rep, which meant everything to him. He wanted his name to ring bells forever when he left the earth.

"What's this clown's name again?" Maxine asked as she loaded her .357.

"Some clown named Carlos." Gruff stood up. "Trust me, this nigga don't want no drama. He gon' give it up with no problem." He stuck his twin 9 mm's in his shoulder holsters. "Come on, Tiger," he said, and him and his partners in crime headed out the door.

"I should be done with this in about two days," Carlos said with a smirk on his face.

"A'ight," Young Mike said. "Just holla at me when you need to see me again."

Young Mike exited the apartment and hit the staircase. As soon as he stepped outside, he quickly reached for the swami on his waist when he saw a loose pit bull walking in his direction. Just as he was about to pull it out, he heard the dog's master yell, "Get over here!" and instantly the dog obeyed the command.

"Yo, put a leash on that muthafucka," Young Mike snarled, his hand still on his swami.

Maxine was about to make a move, but Gruff quickly stopped her. "My bad, fam," he said politely as him, Tiger, and Maxine entered the building.

"You should've let me smoke that clown," Maxine huffed.

Maxine was flat-chested and had no ass. She stood about five foot six inches, was rough-looking, and had short dreads that fell to the back of her neck. And she walked and carried herself like a straight-up man, and didn't take no shit.

"Let's stick to the game plan and get this money," Gruff said, as they went up the staircase.

Carlos sat at his kitchen table bagging up the work he'd just got, while listening to the new Jada Kiss CD, when he saw his front door bust open. Immediately he went for his .380 that rested in the small of his back, but before he could pull his strap, Tiger had already jumped up on top of him, knocking him out the chair.

Gruff put his twin 9s away as he watched Tiger chew up Carlos's arm. "That's enough!" he said sternly, and Tiger backed off.

"Fuck y'all want from me?" Carlos was on his back, clutching his bitten-up arm.

"We want your stash and that work," Gruff said, nodding toward the drugs on the table.

"Man, I ain't got no muthafuckin' money! Just take the work and get the fuck outta here!"

Maxine told him, "I don't think you heard my man correctly. He said, 'We want your stash and that work.'"

"Go fuck yourself!" Carlos growled, still holding his arm. He was scared to death, but his pride wouldn't let him go out like a bitch.

Gruff just shook his head and smirked. "Tiger, get him!"

As Tiger attacked Carlos, Gruff and Maxine searched the apartment for the stash.

Ten minutes later Maxine found a shoebox full of money at the top of the closet. "Jackpot!" she said.

The two returned to the living room to find Carlos laid out dead on the floor.

"Good girl," Gruff said, rubbing Tiger's head. "Come on, baby, let's go clean this blood off your face." He led Tiger to the bathroom, while Maxine packed up all the work.

"Stupid muthafucka!" Maxine yelled at Carlos's dead body as she removed all the drugs from off the kitchen table into a book bag.

Once Gruff and Tiger returned from the bathroom, the trio made their exit.

"What the fuck?" Tone growled when he heard his cell phone ringing. He glanced over at his watch on the nightstand. It read nine-fifteen A.M. "Hello?"

"Wake up, fam," Young Mike said. "Your pops said for you to get over here now."

"A'ight."

Tone quickly got up, took a quick shower, and got dressed.

"Baby, I'll be back in a few," he whispered in Serena's ear, and he kissed her on the cheek.

"Okay, baby, be careful," Serena said, spread out across the bed, her eyes still closed.

Tone pulled the sheet back and slapped her ass before he made his exit.

***

Tone pulled up in front of his father's house and saw a bunch of cars lined up out in the front. "I wonder what's going on now," he said out loud as he exited his vehicle. He tried to prepare himself for something foolish. He knocked on the door and patiently waited for someone to answer the door.

Maine answered the door with a not-so-nice look on his face. "What's good, my nigga?" Maine gave Tone some dap.

Tone stepped inside the house and saw about seven crooked cops and some street soldiers all in the living room. "Fuck going on in here?" he asked, looking around the room.

"Y'all muthafuckas is causing too much fuckin' trouble," Detective Abraham huffed. "That's what's going ·on."

"What you mean, y'all?" Tone asked, confused.

"This nigga Gruff done hit up another one of our spots and killed Carlos. A fuckin' dog chewed his ass to death!"

"Damn! I just seen that nigga as I was leaving Carlos's spot, him, some dike-looking chick, and a big-ass dog," Young Mike announced. "Damn! That was a big-ass dog."

"Well, I got a big-ass bullet with his name on it," Maine said in a matter-of-fact tone.

"Well, you started this muthafuckin' problem, so you better fix it, 'cause we can't afford to keep taking all these fuckin' losses." Detective Abraham turned his gaze on his son. "And you—who the fuck is Big Phil?"

"Some small-time clown. Why? What's up?"

"Word is, this clown suppose to have some money on your head." Detective Abraham shook his head. These problems were the last thing he needed, and felt like dealing with.

"I ain't worried about that clown," Tone said, waving his pops' words off.

"Why the fuck does he have a hit out on you?" Detective Abraham asked.

"I clapped him about a week ago," Tone said nonchalantly.

Detective Abraham turned to the officers in the house. "I need y'all to find this Big Phil cat and bring him to me as soon as possible."

Tone felt his phone vibrate. He looked at his phone and noticed he had a text message from Mya: DROP BY THE HOUSE WHEN YOU GET A CHANCE WE NEED TO TALK!

After he finished reading the message, he stuck his phone back in the case. "We about finished here?" he asked.

"Yeah," Detective Abraham said. "Watch your back out there, son."

"You already know," Tone said, heading for the door.

Mya was sitting Indian-style on the couch in the living room when she heard somebody knocking on the door. She opened the door and stepped to the side so Tone could enter. "Thanks for coming."

"I miss you," Tone said, his eyes roaming her body.

"Well, I can't tell." Mya rolled her eyes. "You ain't even call and check up on a sister or nothing."

"'Cause I been taking care of that business I had told you about," Tone reminded her.

"So how's that been going?" Mya asked, even though she really didn't care. She was still upset about him leaving her to be with another woman.

"So far, so good. So what you need to talk about?"

"I'm pregnant." Mya looked at Tone's face, trying to read his reaction.

"Word?" Tone said, looking her up and down.

"Yes, and I need you back home with me where you belong," Mya whined. "We was suppose to start a family."

"Okay, we can still do all those things right after I get this money."

"Fuck money!" Mya yelled. "We already got enough money!"

Tone looked at her like she was insane. "You can never have enough money."

"So, basically, this shit is never going to stop." Mya shook her head. "I can't believe you."

"Listen, I just need a few more weeks, and then everything will be back to normal, I promise."

"I look stupid to you? You just looked me in my face and told me that you'll never have enough money, so what does that tell me?" Mya couldn't believe what she was hearing. After all they had been through, she felt that Tone owed her more.

"Like I said, I just need a few more weeks, and I'll be back home."

"Fuck that! I need you home now!" Mya yelled. "I'm pregnant, for God's sake!"

"Damn! You talking like you eight months or something. You'll be all right for a few weeks," Tone said, matching Mya's tone.

"You a real piece of shit, you know that?" Mya said, getting all up in Tone's face. "You can't even stop selling drugs to take time out for your family?"

"It's not even—"

"It's time for you to go!" Mya walked over to the door and opened it so Tone could leave.

Tone walked to the door and was about to say something, but Mya quickly stopped him. "Just go," she said, tears streaming down her face. She slammed the door behind him then walked back to her bedroom, where she cried the rest of the night away. She couldn't believe Tone couldn't stop selling drugs and come home. It hurt her even more 'cause, if he wouldn't do it for her, he could at least do it for his child.

Tone walked in the house still thinking about Mya and the news she had just laid on him. He quickly made his way up the steps and into the bedroom, where he found Serena laying across the bed wearing nothing but a pink thong to match her nail polish. The room smelled like fresh fruit. Immediately he knew Serena was fresh out the shower.

"Hey, baby."

"Hey, baby," Serena sang as she jumped in Tone's arms and wrapped her legs around his waist. "Oh my God! I missed you so much," she said, planting kisses all over his face.

"I missed you too, baby," Tone said, forgetting all about Mya.

Serena began massaging Tone's shoulders. "How was your day?"

"Stressful." Tone exhaled a deep breath.

"What's wrong, baby?"

"Been trying to find a new connect," he told her, laying it on thick.

Serena continued to massage his shoulders and back. "How has that been going?"

"Not too good. Nobody seems to have no pure shit. Everything is all stepped on and watered down. But I'ma find something."

"Just be patient, baby. You never know what might happen." Serena gave him a kiss. "You hungry?"

"Yeah. I wanna eat, but I damn sure ain't talking about no food."

Serena blushed. "You so nasty."

Immediately Tone grabbed one of her nice-sized caramel titties and put it in his mouth and hungrily licked and sucked all over it. After about five minutes of that, he quickly pulled off Serena's thong, spread her legs open as far as they could go, and went to work. Tone slowly parted Serena's pretty lips and licked and sucked all over her clitoris, the whole time moaning like it was the best thing he had ever tasted.

Serena lay back and grabbed Tone's head and pushed it all the way in her pussy, twirling her hips and rubbing her wet pussy all over his face.

"Get up, baby. I wanna ride your face!" Serena said in a demanding tone as she got up and tossed Tone on the bed. She quickly mounted his face and continued to get her grind on until she came three times back to back.

As Tone lay on the bed pleasing Serena, he heard a strange noise coming from downstairs. It sounded like someone dropped a glass or something. "Hold on, baby," he said, interrupting Serena's ride.

"No, baby. Please don't stop. I'm about to come again."

"Nah, hold on!" Tone said in a strong whisper, sliding from up under Serena's wet pussy.

He quickly grabbed his 9 mm from off the dresser and walked out into the hallway. He tiptoed over by the steps and looked over the rail. He saw around eight to eleven men wearing ski masks creeping through out the house. *Fuck!* He tiptoed back into the bedroom. "Shhh." He placed his index finger on his lips as he handed Serena the 9 mm he held. "Here, take this and get under the bed."

Serena didn't say a word. She just grabbed the gun and got under the bed butt naked and all. Tone quickly ran over to his closet and grabbed his AR-15 and hit the lights. He placed his back up against the wall and waited patiently. Seconds later, he heard footsteps slowly creeping up the steps. On a silent count of three, he sprang from behind the wall firing.

PAT, TAT, TAT, TAT, TAT!

Tone watched as the bullets from his AR-15 sent five of the gunmen back down the stairs. Immediately the other gunmen returned fire, decorating Tone's wall with about thirty-five bullets. Tone stayed low as he winked to Serena, who lay under the bed, looking scared to death.

Once the gunfire stopped, Tone quickly sprang from around the corner and fired his assault rifle again, killing two more of the gunmen.

The gunmen returned fire again. Tone reloaded his weapon as he heard sirens getting louder and louder. He knew the cops would be coming soon because of the nice neighborhood the condo was in. Suddenly he heard the gunmen scrambling to get up out the house.

"Yo!" Tone called out to Serena. "Get some clothes on quick. The cops will be here any second," he said as he slowly headed downstairs.

"Baby, where you going?" Serena asked, panic all in her voice.

"Downstairs," he yelled over his shoulder, "to make sure all them muthafuckas is up outta here."

"Wait up. I'm coming with you," Serena said, quickly tagging along, and the two quickly made their way downstairs.

The first thing Tone did when he got downstairs was turn on the lights.

Just then a big, strong-looking cop kicked in the front door. "Drop the fuckin' gun!" he yelled, his .357 aimed at Tone's head.

Tone slowly laid the AR-15 on the carpet and put his hands up in surrender. Just then an army of cops and detectives busted up in the house. The cops threw Tone and Serena to the floor and cuffed them.

"Muthafuckas broke into my house!" Tone yelled from the floor. "Why the fuck y'all got me handcuffed?"

The lead detective came downstairs holding four guns, including the AR-15. "I hope you have a permit for all of these." He shook his head. "Get these two animals out of here!" he ordered. "Seven dead bodies. I hope they give this creep the death penalty."

Chapter 8

The C.O. pushed Tone inside the room. "You got twenty minutes."

"Bitch-ass nigga!" Tone mumbled under his breath as he entered the room and saw his father and his lawyer, Mr. Goldberg, sitting at a small table.

Before Tone could even sit down, his father shot to his feet. "Didn't I tell you to watch your back? You never fuckin' listen. You think you fuckin' know everything."

"What is you talking about?" Tone replied. "You said to watch my back, and that's what I did."

"You stupid muthafucka! What you think we got goons and soldiers for?"

"What I need security for when I got a gun? Plus, I don't want muthafuckas all up in my house and following me around twenty-four seven."

"Okay. Well, you can have the police follow you around and tell you what to do, since you wanna be stupid," Detective Abraham barked. "I told you about trying to be tough. All tough niggas is sitting in jail. You gotta be smart. I taught you better than that."

"Can't I beat this case on self-defense? I mean, they did break into my house."

"No," Mr. Goldberg replied. "You can beat the murders on self-defense, but you going to have to eat those gun charges."

"You can't get all that shit thrown out?" Tone asked, a defeated look on his face.

"I'm afraid not," Mr. Goldberg told him. "The guns were illegal, and the serial numbers were all scratched off."

"Fuck!" Tone buried his face in his hands. "How much time I'm looking at?"

"Five years, but you'll be out in three and a half if you don't get into no trouble while you're in there," Mr. Goldberg informed him.

"Next time use your head!" Detective Abraham stormed out the room, slamming the door behind him.

"When am I getting the fuck up outta here?"

"Tomorrow morning when you see the judge. I don't see why he wouldn't give you bail."

"A'ight. What's up with Serena?" Tone asked.

"She'll be released tomorrow if you say those guns were yours."

"Yeah, I'll let 'em know tomorrow."

The C.O. came busting in the room. "Time's up!"

Tone shook Mr. Goldberg's hand as he followed the C.O. back to his cell.

Three days later Tone was let out on bail. He stepped out the jail with a mean look on his face. Young Mike and Serena were leaning on a car, waiting for him.

"What's good, convict?" Young Mike said playfully as he gave Tone a pound.

"Fuckin' crackers always tryin'a get some time out of a nigga," he huffed. He gave Serena a big hug and kiss.

"Don't even worry about it, baby. We gonna be fine," Serena assured him.

Before long, Young Mike pulled up in front of Tone's crib and put the car in park. "Yo, y'all sure y'all wanna stay here? I can drop y'all off at a hotel if you want."

"Nah, we good here. Good looking though," Tone said, and him and Serena slid out the car and headed inside the condo.

"Damn!" Serena said when she saw all the bulletholes in the wall. The night they had got arrested she hadn't noticed them.

"We can go to a hotel if you want," Tone told her.

"Nah, I'm good." She noticed the sad look on Tone's face. "What's wrong, baby?"

"Everything is all fucked up now. That's what's wrong. I don't have a connect, and now muthafuckas ain't gonna wanna fuck with me while I'm dealing with this case. So many niggas is snitching, niggas gon' think I'm tryin'a set 'em up or some other crazy shit."

"Don't worry. Everything is going to be okay," Serena said, rubbing Tone's back.

"How?" Tone yelled. "I don't have no connect. No connect means no money!"

"Well, when I go back home tomorrow, I'll talk to my uncle and see what I can do for you, baby. Okay?"

"That's okay, baby. I don't really want you getting involved in this shit," Tone said, lying through his teeth.

"Baby, trust me, it's okay. My father has a straight line to where the shit comes from." She paused. "Only problem is, he don't do business with blacks, so I'm going to have to talk to my uncle. He's cooler."

"Okay, baby. As long you ain't gon' get in no trouble, then I'm cool with it." Tone pulled her in close for a hug. "If something happened to you, I would never forgive myself."

"Everything is going to be fine. I'ma go back home for a few days, talk to my uncle and set everything up. You don't worry about nothing. All I need you to do is relax and watch how a real bitch holds her man down," Serena said, putting on her gangsta face.

"You too cute to be acting tough like that." Tone lifted her chin for a kiss.

"I gotta hold my man down."

"Oh, so I'm your man now?" Tone asked with a smirk.

"You muthafuckin' right," Serena replied as she accepted his kiss.

"And I'ma make sure my man is all right," she said, every word coming from her heart.

After the two showered, they had sex all night and all morning until it was time for Serena to leave.

"You know I'm gonna miss you, right?" Tone said.

"I'll only be gone for a week, and I'm gonna miss you like crazy while I'm gone."

"You just make sure you call me and keep me close," Tone said as he saw Serena's cab pull up. "And call me as soon as you get there."

"You know I am, baby." Serena gave Tone some tongue before she went and slid in the back seat of the cab, which Tone watched until it was no longer in sight.

Big Phil sat at his kitchen table counting money when he heard somebody knocking at his door. He quickly grabbed the TEC-9 from off the table and walked toward the door. "Who is it?"

"Open up the fuckin' door," the voice on the other end barked.

Big Phil opened up the door and stepped to the side so Gruff and Maxine could enter. "I'm glad y'all could make it on such short notice."

"How many exits you got in this muthafucka?" Gruff asked, just in case something jumped off.

"Just the front door and the back door. Why? What's up?" Big Phil asked.

"No reason," Gruff said. "So what's up? You said you wanted to talk business, so talk."

"I'ma cut straight to the chase," Big Phil said, pouring himself a drink. "I want to hire you to do a job for me."

"What kind of job?"

"I need somebody dead." Big Phil downed his drink in one gulp.

"I'm not no hit man," Gruff said quickly.

"Not even for twenty grand?" Big Phil snatched the money off the table and handed it to Gruff.

"Who we gotta hit?" Gruff asked, stuffing the money in both of his back pockets.

"Some bitch-ass nigga name Tone." Big Phil started giving Gruff and Maxine a quick rundown.

"I heard of him." Gruff heard some noise coming from outside the door. "What the fuck is that?" He quickly pulled out his twin 9s from his shoulder holsters.

Bam!

The front door came crashing in, followed by three armed police officers.

"Pull over right here," Detective Abraham ordered as he loaded his shotgun. "That's the muthafucka's house right there," he said as he slid out the van.

A white racist cop named Tom said, "I'm shooting anything that moves when we get up in here!"

"Listen, we gon' go in here, smoke this clown, and be on our way. Simple as that." Detective Abraham looked at his men to make sure he was understood before they reached the front of the house. Tone may have got on his nerves, but that was still his son, and anyone who tried to harm him had to die.

Altogether there were six officers. Three officers took the front door, while Detective Abraham, Tom, and another officer headed toward the back.

The biggest officer of the three grabbed the battering ram and quickly busted down the door on the second try. "Freeze! Police!" was all he got to say before he collapsed to the floor covered in his own blood.

Gruff had quickly aimed his twin 9s at the door and fired two shots. *POW! POW!* Both shots hit the first officer in the stomach.

The next officer came running inside holding a shotgun in his hand. Before he could even get a shot off, Gruff had already shot him three times, and Maxine finished him off with a shot to the head with her .357 Magnum.

Maxine quickly held up one finger, letting Gruff know that one more officer was outside the door. She slowly eased her way toward the door. As Gruff eased his way toward the front door, he heard a loud *BOOM!* then watched as the back door flew off its hinges. Big Phil immediately opened fire on the back door, not caring who he hit.

The third cop finally entered the front door firing recklessly, hitting everything but his intended targets. Maxine quickly dropped him with three shots to the chest.

"We out!" Gruff said as he ran out the front door with Maxine close on his heels.

"Yo, wait up!" Big Phil yelled as he fired a few more rounds at the back door. Then he ran out the front door behind Gruff and Maxine.

Detective Abraham ran inside the house with his shotgun in hand, ready to tear up some shit. "They ran out the front!" he yelled, and him, Tom, and the other officer headed out the front door in pursuit of the gunmen.

"Yo, wait up," Big Phil said out of breath as he finally caught up to Gruff and Maxine.

Immediately Gruff turned and placed the barrel of his 9 mm to Big Phil's head and pulled the trigger. He didn't even watch his body drop as he slid in the driver's seat of their stolen hooptie.

"Why the fuck you kill Phil for?" Maxine looked back to make sure they wasn't being followed.

"Cops came to his house. That means eventually they was going to find him, and you know he ain't going down for killing three cops," Gruff said, as he hopped on the highway.

Maxine thought about it for a second. "You right."

"Damn!" Detective Abraham said when they reached Big Phil's dead body.

"Looks like somebody beat us to the punch," Tom said with a smirk.

Detective Abraham watched the getaway car bend the corner at full speed. "I guess so."

Chapter 9

Tone took a deep breath before he exited his car. He walked up to the front door and knocked on it.

Mya answered the door, her smile quickly turning into a frown. "What do you want?"

"We need to talk. Can I come in?"

"Now is not a good time. I got company."

"Damn! How you got another nigga all up in the crib while you pregnant?"

"Don't come up in here judging me. Besides, he's just my friend. I don't go around fucking anything that moves, like somebody else I know." Mya rolled her eyes.

"Whatever. What we gon' do about this baby?"

"What you mean, *we*?" Mya said, a confused look on her face. "I'm gonna have my baby and take care of it. That's what I'm going to do. I don't know what you gon' do."

"So it's like that?"

"Just like that, until you get your priorities together."

Just as Tone was about to reply, a man wearing a suit came up behind Mya. "Is everything okay over here?" he asked.

To Tone, he looked like a businessman or a lawyer. Tone stared coldly at the man. "And if it ain't?"

"I'm calling the police." The man disappeared back inside the house.

"Don't come over here starting no shit," Mya said.

Tone looked at Mya with disgust as he turned and walked back to his car. Once he got behind the wheel, he heard his cell phone ringing. He looked at the caller ID and saw that it was Maine. "What's good?" he answered.

"Where you at?"

"Out. Why? What's up?"

"Shoot over to my crib real quick," Maine said, ending the call.

An hour later Tone stepped inside Maine's apartment and saw guns all over the place. "You about to go to war with somebody?" he asked half-jokingly.

"Just got the word on where Gruff lives," Maine said with a smile. "My leg is fully healed. Now it's time to get back to business."

"So what you called me for?"

"I wanted you to take a ride with me."

"Nigga, you know I'm out on bail right now. I can't be getting into more shit."

"Nigga, you ain't gotta do shit. Just ride with me and keep a nigga company. You act like I asked you to pop somebody's head off in broad daylight."

"A'ight, let's go."

Tone and Maine headed out the door. Tone knew it was a bad idea but still decided to go along anyway.

"So how did you get this fool's address?"

"Got it from a fiend," Maine said, quickly backing out of his driveway.

"You sure you shouldn't've brought a few more guys with you?" Tone asked. "I heard this fool even sleeps with his hand on his gun."

"Fuck him!" Maine spat. "That nigga gonna die with his hand on his gun tonight too."

"I was just saying."

"Nigga, I'm a one-man army," Maine boasted, as he stepped on the gas.

"How did you learn to shoot so good?" Maxine asked as she sat on the bench with Gruff.

"Practice," Gruff answered quickly. He was watching Tiger run around in the grass. "I stayed in the hood range, until my aim was where I needed it to be."

"I gotta work on my shit."

"Practice makes perfect." Gruff noticed an all-black Audi pull in front of his apartment. Immediately he knew it was trouble. "Who that?" he asked Maxine as they watched from a block away two men wearing all-black kick open their front door and enter their apartment.

"I don't know." Maxine pulled out her .357. "Let's go find out."

"Nah," Gruff said quickly. "Patience."

Maine kicked the front door open and quickly rushed inside the crib, Tone on his heels. The two searched the whole apartment and found it empty.

"Filthy-ass niggas," Maine said, looking around the apartment.

In the living room was nothing but a dirty-looking mattress on the floor, the bathroom smelled like shit, and the bedroom looked like an animal lived in it.

Maine snatched open the fridge and just shook his head in disgust. Inside was a box of baking soda and a light bulb. "Bum-ass nigga!" he said to himself, mad that the house was empty. "You wanna wait for the nigga to come home?"

"Fuck outta here!" Tone said, his nose wrinkled up from the foul odor of the apartment. "I ain't staying in here another second," he said as he exited the apartment.

"Oh shit." Gruff smiled. "That's Tone right there."

Maxine stared coldly at the two men exiting their apartment. "Who's that?"

"The nigga Big Phil had hired us to kill." Gruff watched Maine pull out some kind of machine gun and spray up his apartment before fleeing the scene. "At first I wasn't gonna fill the contract, since I already killed Big Phil, but now we gonna kill these niggas for fun."

"The sooner the better," Maxine added.

"That was a nice little message I sent back there, right?" Maine said, glancing over at Tone.

"I guess," Tone said in a bored tone.

"What you mean, you guess?" Maine said, clearly upset.

"I mean, you should've waited until you ran into to him to send a message. This clown probably got a million enemies. How's he gonna know it came from you?"

"Good point," Maine said as he pulled up in Detective Abraham's driveway.

"Why did you bring me here?" Tone asked.

Maine let the engine die. "Your pops texted me and said he wanted to see both of us."

They stepped inside the house and saw Detective Abraham sitting in his usual seat at the kitchen table, having a drink. "How nice of you two to show up," he said, a smirk on his face.

"What's up, Pops? I heard you wanted to see me."
Tone gave his father a hug.

"Yeah. What's the status with you and that chick?"

"She's out of town right now working on that, as we
speak," Tone told his father.

"So is it a definite?" Detective Abraham asked excitedly.

"Won't know until she gets back."

"When does she get back?" Detective Abraham asked.

"In a few days," Tone answered.

"You been keeping out of trouble?"

Tone lied, "Of course, I have."

"I don't want you doing nothing, you hear?" Detective Abraham warned. "You out on bail and don't need
no more trouble."

"My hands are clean," Tone said, throwing up his
hands in surrender.

"Keep 'em clean," Detective Abraham said as he turned
and headed up the steps. "Y'all can let y'all selves out," he
called down from the top of the steps.

Maine pulled up in front of Tone's house and noticed
someone sitting on his doorstep. "Yo, who the fuck is
that sitting on ya muthafuckin' doorstep?"

"I have no idea," Tone said, squinting his eyes to get
a better look. He pulled his .40-cal from his waistband.
"I can't tell who that is from here."

Both men hopped out the vehicle, their guns drawn,
and approached the man. Tone immediately lowered
his gun when he saw that the man sitting on his doorstep 'sleep was his brother Malcolm.

"You good?" Maine asked, looking down at Malcolm
in disgust.

"Yeah, I'm straight. I'ma holla at you tomorrow," Tone said, embarrassed.

Once Maine pulled off, Tone shook his brother. "Nigga, wake the fuck up!" he yelled.

"Oh! Hey, Tone. I was looking for you," Malcolm said, smiling and showing his rotten teeth.

"Fuck is you doing on my doorstep?" Tone opened the front door and shoved Malcolm inside.

Malcolm whined, "Your big brother needs a little favor."

"No more favors!" Tone yelled. "You need to kick this shit. This ain't for you."

"This my last night getting high," Malcolm said with a smile. "I'm done with all this shit after tonight. All I need from you is fifty dollars, and I'll be on my way."

Tone knew he was lying, but for some reason he gave him the money anyway. "Here, muthafucka." He shoved the money in his brother's hand. "If I hear about you getting high after tonight, we no longer family. When I see you, I will walk right past you like I don't know you."

"Thanks, Tone. I promise I won't let you down." Malcolm leaned in for a hug.

"Get yourself together," Tone said sternly, giving his brother a hug.

"You the only family I got left," Malcolm said as he quickly turned and exited his brother's home in a hurry to get high.

Tone watched as his brother disappeared into the night. All he could do was hope and pray that his brother kept his word, but deep down inside he knew his brother was fighting a battle he couldn't win.

***

For the entire ride home all Maine could think about was what he was gonna do to Gruff when he finally bumped into him. When he stepped foot inside his house, he noticed the bathroom light was on, but he clearly remembered turning it off.

Immediately Maine pulled out his . 380 with the silencer already on the end of the barrel. As he slowly crept up the steps with a two-handed grip on his weapon, the mystery person exited the bathroom in a hurry.

Maine quickly lowered his gun when he saw who exited his bathroom. "Fuck is you doing here?"

"Baby, I was trying to surprise you," Monique sang, her arms open for a hug.

Maine's hand quickly shot out and stopped Monique from hugging him. "Didn't I tell you not to come back?"

"I'm sorry, daddy, but I missed you," Monique whined. "I was just trying to surprise you before you got home."

"Well, thanks for the surprise. Now put your clothes on and get out," Maine said, trying not to look at Monique's stripper outfit. She was wearing red fishnet stockings, tall red hooker boots, and a red bra.

"Can I have one more chance, daddy? Please?"

"Nah, you gotta go."

"Pleeeeease?" Monique purred. She grabbed on Maine's belt and began unbuckling it.

Next thing you know, Maine found himself fucking Monique's mouth like it was a pussy. Monique held on to Maine's dick with two hands, while she allowed him to have his way with her mouth, until he finally exploded in it.

"Fuck!" Maine cursed out loud, mad that he could never resist Monique's touch.

"I'm sorry, daddy. I promise I'll be the best girlfriend in the world from now on."

Monique hugged Maine and rested her head on his chest, and for the rest of the night, the two had wild make-up sex.

Chapter 10

"I don't know about this," Lopez said, rubbing his chin.

Serena pressed as the two sat in the restaurant. "Please, Uncle Lopez."

"You know me and your father don't fuck with them niggers," Lopez reminded her. "They can't be trusted."

"I know the rules, but trust me, Tone is different," Serena said. "Just start him out with ten, and see how he does. I promise you, he won't let you down."

"Too risky. Plus, nobody's gonna want to drop that off to your friend." Lopez laughed, shaking his head.

"They can just drop it off to me, and I'll give it to him. That way no one can get in trouble. If anybody gets in trouble, it'll be me."

"You must really love this guy," Lopez said in deep thought. "I tell you what—I'll deal with you and you only, but only on one condition."

"Anything!" Serena said, the biggest smile on her face.

"If your father finds out, you didn't get this from me," Lopez said seriously. "Even though I'm his brother, I know for a fact he'll kill me."

"My lips are sealed."

"Okay, when you get back to New York, call me, and I'll have one of my partners get in touch with you and you only. If you ever bring someone else with you, the deal is off. Understand?"

"Understood," Serena said, and her and her uncle shook hands.

Monique sat on the couch watching re-runs of *Martin* when she heard the house phone ring. She quickly picked it up on the second. "Hello?"

"Hey, baby. What you doing?" Maine asked.

"Nothing. Just sitting here watching *Martin*, and missing you," Monique told him. "When you coming home, daddy?"

"On my way now, baby. I should be there in about fifteen minutes."

"Okay, baby, hurry up 'cause I—"

Before Monique could finish her sentence, she heard a loud *BOOOOOM!* then saw the front door swing open. Monique saw a man wearing a hoodie standing in the doorway, a smirk on his lips, and behind him was a rough-looking chick with a mean look on her face, both holding big guns.

"Oooh shit!" Monique screamed. She hopped up off the couch with quickness and flew up the steps. As she ran, she remembered that Maine always kept an emergency gun under the mattress.

Gruff stood in the doorway with the same smirk on his face. He looked down at Tiger. "Go get her!" he commanded.

Monique looked back when reached the middle of the steps, only to see a vicious pit bull making its way up the stairs. She panicked and tripped on the last step. She hopped up off the floor quickly but not quick enough. Tiger jumped on her back, tackling her to the floor, then bit down into her neck, growling. Gruff and Maxine just looked on as Tiger ripped Monique to pieces.

Gruff lit up a Newport. "Check the bedroom for a safe."

"I got you," Maxine replied as she headed toward the bedroom. She walked right past Tiger while she was still chewing Monique's dead body.

Five minutes later Maxine came back downstairs.

"Bum-ass nigga ain't have no safe, but he did have twenty grand in his drawer," she said, tapping her pocket.

"Very good," Gruff said, and him and Maxine exited the house. "Tiger, let's go," he yelled over his shoulder, and the dog ran to his master.

"Hello!" Maine was still yelling into the phone since he'd heard a loud boom and Monique screaming to the top of her lungs. He continued to listen as he heard Monique hit the floor then heard the sound of some kind of animal or something.

Immediately he dropped his phone as he put the pedal to the metal, weaving in and out of lanes, driving about 90 miles an hour. Nine minutes later, he came to a skidding stop in front of his house. He hopped out his car, his .380 already in his hand, and busted through the front door holding his gun with a two-handed grip.

Straightaway, he spotted Monique's body at the top of the steps. "Ah, hell naw," he said out loud as he reached the top of the steps and looked down at Monique's half-eaten body. "Muthafuckas!" he shouted as he turned his head away. He rushed downstairs and dialed 9-1-1 from the house phone. "I need an ambulance now!" he said into the receiver before hanging up and heading out the door.

Tone stepped out the shower, wrapped himself in a towel, and grabbed his .45 from off the toilet seat.

Someone was banging on his door, and he wasn't expecting company.

Bang! Bang! Then there was a pause.

Bang!

Tone looked through the peephole and quickly lowered his gun. He opened the door in a hurry. "Hey, what you doing here?"

"I came to see my muthafuckin' man." Serena smiled as she closed the door behind her.

"Ya ass almost got shot, banging like the fuckin' police." Tone held up his gun for Serena to see.

"Well, you had me out here knocking for like ten minutes. I had to make sure you heard me." Serena smiled as she removed Tone's towel from around his waist. "Did y'all miss me?" she asked, looking down at Tone's dick.

"Come find out," Tone shot back as he walked to the bedroom, ass naked.

When Serena reached the bedroom, she quickly stripped out of her clothes and slid into Tone's arms.

"I missed you so fuckin' much while I was gone," she said in between kisses, jerking his dick, making it brick-hard.

Tone quickly pulled away from Serena's kisses, bending down and scooping her up into the air like he was about to body-slam her. Next thing Serena knew, she was upside down in the air. She immediately locked her legs around the back of Tone's head as she felt his tongue sloppily massage her clitoris.

Tone buried his face in Serena's pussy, forcing her to come for him yet again. Serena, still hanging upside down, moaned as she grabbed Tone's dick with two hands and started sucking the shit out of it.

Tone felt his knees weakening each time Serena's head bobbed up and down on his dick, so he quickly laid her down on the bed.

"Come ride ya dick." He lay back and watched Serena climb up on top of him, reach back, and place his manhood inside of her.

"Damn!" Serena moaned as she planted her hands on Tone's chest and bounced her ass up and on Tone's dick like this was the last time she would ever get dick again in her life.

Just as Tone was getting ready to come, he heard loud knocks coming from his front door again.

Bang! Bang! Bang!

Tone quickly sat up and grabbed his sweat pants from off the floor and put them on. Then he grabbed his .45 and headed to the peephole to see who was outside banging on his door. Once he saw who it was, he lowered his gun and unlocked the door.

"Yo, they fuckin' killed her!" Maine said loudly as he stormed up in the house. "They fuckin' killed her!"

"Calm down," Tone began. "Killed who?"

"Monique." Maine broke down crying. "They fuckin' her killed her."

"Who killed her?" Tone asked.

"Gruff," Maine said, his head buried in his hands.

Serena peeked her head from out the room. "Is everything okay, baby?"

"Yes, baby, everything is fine," Tone said, waving her back into the room. "Now what happened?"

"When I got home"—Maine paused to wipe his face— "I saw her body laying at the top of the steps. When I finally reached up top, I saw her body all chewed up into little pieces."

"Into little pieces?" Tone asked, making sure he heard correctly.

"Into little pieces, like she was a piece of meat."

"We gon' have to hurry up and catch these muthafuckas," Tone said out loud. "These niggas must think they on some wild wild west shit."

"I'm about to turn it up out here on these streets," Maine said with watery eyes. "These muthafuckas wanna play, so now we gon' show them how it's done."

"Good girl," Gruff said, rubbing the back of Tiger's head as she chewed down on a chicken bone.

Maxine laughed, thinking back on the situation. "She ate that bitch the fuck up."

"Tiger don't play that shit."

Since she was a puppy, Gruff had been training Tiger to be a killing machine. Now, after all of those years of training, it was finally paying off.

"So what's next for us?"

"Tone," Gruff said in a neutral voice.

"How we gon' get at him?"

Gruff told her, "Easy. By going after his money."

"You already know I don't give a fuck!" Maxine said in her manly voice. "We going to take these clowns out one by one."

Tone sat on the couch counting money when he heard his front door being unlocked. "What the fuck!" He quickly grabbed his .45 that rested on the coffee table.

"Hey, baby," Serena said, walking through the front door with a duffel bag over her shoulder.

"Damn!" Tone placed his .45 back down on the coffee table. "I forgot I gave you a key."

Serena shook her head. "How you forget you gave me a key?" She leaned down and kissed Tone on his lips.

"My bad." Tone looked at the duffel bag on the floor and motioned his head toward it. "What's that?"

"Oh, I had to go pick up something nice for my man." Serena smiled.

Tone huffed. "Didn't I tell you I don't want you buying me nothing?"

"Oh, shut up and open it."

Tone lifted up the duffel bag and sat it on the coffee table. When he opened it, his eyes lit up. Inside was ten pure-white kilos. "Where did you get this from?"

"Why you all in my business?" Serena said playfully as she slid in Tone's arms. "Did I do good, baby?"

"You did excellent, baby," Tone said excitedly. "Now I gotta go out and get this money."

"Let ya baby ease your mind first," Serena said as she slid down to her knees.

"Awww shit!" Tone moaned as he felt Serena's full lips on his dick.

Serena made sure she made her mouth extra wet just like he liked it.

Once Tone felt himself about to come, he quickly began fucking Serena's mouth like it was a pussy, until he exploded in her mouth.

Serena walked over to the garbage and spat before she spoke. "Now go handle your business," she said with a smile on her face.

"I love you, baby," Tone said as he threw the duffel bag over his shoulder. "I won't be back too late."

Serena watched Tone walk out the house. "Just be careful."

"It's about damn time," Detective Abraham said, looking at his son. "So is this shit going to work?"

Tone told him, "Basically, they don't fuck with black people, so we gon' have to go through her."

"So what's wrong with that?"

"It's Mya," Tone said in a low tone. "She's pregnant."

"So what's the problem?"

"She don't want nothing to do with me no more."
Tone paused. "That part doesn't bother me. I just
didn't want to end on bad terms like that, you know?
Especially when everything was going so good."

"That's life," Detective Abraham said in a harsh tone.
"When you suppose to be going to do this time?" he
said, quickly changing the subject. The part he didn't
tell his son at the beginning was, once Serena got the
connect, he wasn't going to able to stop dealing with
her 'cause, if he did, she would no longer let her connect supply them.

"In three months. And I ain't in no rush," Tone said,
mad that he had to give up his freedom for such a long
time.

"That three and a half years gonna fly by," Detective
Abraham said as if it was no big deal.

On that note, Tone gave his father a hug and made
his exit.

Chapter 11

Young Mike stood inside the stash house bagging up the new product, along with a few other workers. Of course, he didn't have to help bag up, but the faster the work was bagged up, the faster everyone could get out of there.

"Y'all niggas, hurry up, so we can get up outta here," Young Mike said as he went to the bathroom. He had been having to take a shit all day, and now was the perfect time for him to handle his business.

The rest of the workers continued to bag up, until they heard something or somebody tapping at the back door.

"Go answer the muthafuckin' door!" Harlem said.

One of the other workers shot back, "Nigga, you answer the door," never looking up from the product on the table.

"Fuck it! Whoever it is just won't be getting in." Harlem shrugged his shoulders as he stood up to stretch.

A little while later, there was a loud gunshot, followed by the doorknob and lock from the back door hitting the ground.

Gruff kicked open the back door and swept his Uzi through the air, popping any and everything in his path.

Harlem quickly bent the corner heading down the hallway. A few of the other workers tried to return fire, but it was no use. They were completely caught off guard.

While Gruff reloaded his weapon, Maxine covered him as she eased her way inside the apartment, her MAC-11 gripped tight. In less than ten seconds Gruff had reloaded his weapon.

Young Mike's whole body shook when he heard the loud roar of a machine gun being fired inside the house. "Oh shit!" He said loudly, hopping up off the toilet. He pulled his pants up without wiping and grabbed his 9 mm from off the sink. He cracked the door and saw Harlem with his back up against the wall holding two handguns.

Harlem mouthed the words, "I'm banging out."

Young Mike nodded his head as he continued to peek out the bathroom door. Once he saw a figure, he snatched open the bathroom door, stuck his arm out, and let off four shots—*POW! POW! POW! POW!*—and quickly closed it back.

Seconds later, about fifteen shots came ripping through the door, followed by little pieces of wood flying all over the place.

Harlem stayed with his back up against the wall until he heard the gunfire stop. Once he felt the time was right, he swiftly sprang from behind the wall firing. Two of his shots hit Maxine in the chest, causing her to stumble backwards until she hit the floor.

Before Harlem could take cover behind the wall, Gruff shot him in the shoulder, causing him to drop both of his guns.

"Awww shit!" Harlem screamed out like a bitch as he jogged into the back room.

Young Mike stood in the bathroom not knowing what was going on. He'd heard mad shots being fired, a woman's scream then a man's scream, followed by more gunshots.

"Fuck it!" Young Mike silently counted to three, and snatched opened the bathroom door but didn't see nobody. He slowly stepped out the bathroom, looked to his left and saw Harlem clutching his shoulder in the bedroom. He ignored Harlem and continued to inch his way down the hallway. He reached the end of the hallway and quickly turned the corner with a two-handed grip on his 9 mm. "Fuck!" He saw all the workers laid out and blood all over the place. He ran to the back room where Harlem was. "Come on, we gotta go," Young Mike said in a fast-paced voice.

"I clapped that bitch up," Harlem said, a smile on his face.

Young Mike didn't reply. He just threw Harlem's arm around his neck and helped him out the crib.

"Come on, you all right?" Gruff whispered in Maxine's ear as he tossed her in the back seat of their ride and peeled off at a high speed. "How you feeling?" he asked, his eyes on the road.

Maxine clutched the vest that was strapped to her chest. "My fuckin' ribs are broke!"

"You gon' be all right," Gruff assured her. Just then he saw a Honda Accord tailing him. "What the fuck?" he said out loud.

"You can't be scared to die out here in these streets," Maine said, coaching a new soldier they had just recruited. "You strapped right now?"

The young soldier was happy to finally be on a winning team. "Yeah."

"Never leave home without that shit, you hear?" Maine stopped at the red light and looked over at the kid. "What's your name anyway?"

"Everybody calls me Smith."

"Fuck kind of name is Smith?"

Smith revealed the handle of his gun. "They call me that because I always got my Smith and Wesson on me."

Maine smiled. "I like that."

As Maine pulled up on the stash house block, he saw a car driving recklessly across the lawn, attempting to make a getaway. Instantly he recognized the driver. "Yo, hold on!" Maine yelled. He quickly made a sharp right turn, following the man he had been waiting to come in contact with for weeks.

"Hold on, we got some company." Gruff pulled one of his 9 mm's with his free hand, while he kept his other hand on the wheel. He watched closely through his rearview mirror as the all-black Honda sped up on his side. Then he quickly flung his arm out the window and let off three shots.

POW! POW! POW!

Maine and Smith ducked down as three shots exploded through the front windshield. Smith then rolled down his window and returned fire, and Gruff quickly ducked down as he swerved three lanes over and sped up.

"They still behind us?" Maxine asked, pain in her voice.

"Yeah."

Gruff took the next exit. When he reached the intersection, he slowly made an illegal right turn, clogging up the intersection, causing several other cars to blow their horns.

"Fuck!" Maine cursed when he reached the clogged-up intersection and saw Gruff making a clean getaway.

Just then, through his rearview mirror, he saw flashing lights coming in their direction at a fast speed. "Awww shit! Five-O!" He slid out of the driver's seat and took off on foot.

Smith hopped out the car and took off on foot in the opposite direction, hoping the cops would chase

Maine, but today wasn't his lucky day 'cause, when he turned around, he saw two white officers chasing him with a K-9.

It didn't take long for the K-9 to grab a hold of Smith's arm and drag him down to the ground, where the officers then handcuffed him.

Young Mike exited the front door of the house struggling to hold up Harlem. Before they could even reach the curb, he saw mad police cars pull up to the scene. Young Mike looked at Harlem and quickly pushed him off and ran back inside the house, where he hopped over all the dead bodies and ran out the back door.

The police quickly tackled Harlem, bending his injured arm behind his back as they cuffed him and tossed him in the back seat of a squad car. The rest of the officers then quickly entered the house, to witness a scene full of drugs and dead bodies.

Chapter 12

Detective Abraham stepped inside the house and shook his head in disgust as he looked around at the shell cases and blood all over the place.

A uniformed officer called him over, "Detective, over here."

"What do we got?"

"Looks like a robbery gone bad," the officer said. "But we did capture two of the suspects."

"For real?" Detective Abraham asked, wide-eyed.

"Yeah, two hotheads," the officer said. "One even had a bullet in his shoulder."

"Well, I'ma get down to the station and try to crack those two suspects." Detective Abraham turned and headed toward the door.

As soon as Detective Abraham got back in his car, he pulled out his cell phone and dialed Maine's number.

"Yeah," Maine answered.

"What the fuck is going on? And why the fuck didn't anybody tell me that shit got fucked up at the spot?" Detective Abraham yelled.

"Listen, man, shit happened mad quick. I barely even got away."

"I don't give a fuck!" Detective Abraham yelled. "Shit gets fucked up, you check in."

"You right, my bad."

"So who fucked up our shit?"

"That nigga Gruff," Maine said. "I spoke to Young Mike, and he told me that Harlem shot the bitch that be with that nigga."

"A'ight, I'll figure this shit out, but next time, as soon as shit hits the fan, I better be notified," Detective Abraham said, ending the call.

Detective Abraham reached the station and walked straight up to the desk officer. "Where's the two idiots that got brought in for the drug deal gone wrong?"

"Cell four," the officer answered.

Detective Abraham walked down toward Cell four. "I need someone down here to open up this cell for me," he yelled out, and a female officer came and opened it up.

"Thanks." Detective Abraham waited for the woman to walk back down the hall before he entered the cell. "You two muthafuckas better keep y'all mouths shut," he said in a strong whisper. "I'ma do what I can to get y'all the least time as possible. Y'all just keep quiet and shut the fuck up!" Pissed, he walked out the cell and closed it shut behind him. This was the third spot already that Gruff had hit, all because Maine wanted to start some shit.

"So I got up outta there as fast as possible," Young Mike told Tone as the two sat at the kitchen table having a drink.

"Damn! So this Gruff nigga came through again?" Tone asked. "Fuck, this nigga ain't got shit else better to do?"

"I don't know, but I know Harlem popped up the bitch who always be with him."

Tone poured himself another shot. "This nigga is starting to be a pain in the ass."

"Who the fuck is this nigga?" Young Mike asked.

"Some bum-ass stickup kid with nothing to live for," Tone answered quickly. "I been trying to be cool since I caught this case, but—fuck all that—I might have to get back on my shit."

"You gon' have to chill. It's about to be mad hot out here. Too many bodies been dropping lately."

"You right."

"I'm about to get up outta here." Young Mike stood up to leave. "Just wanted to touch base with you first."

"Good looking," Tone said as he gave Young Mike a pound and a hug. "I appreciate that. Listen, I want you to lay low for a couple of days, a'ight."

"I got you," Young Mike said as he turned and made his exit.

Just then Serena entered the kitchen. "Is everything okay?"

"Nah. This nigga Gruff keep on sticking his nose in our business."

"What did he do now?" Serena asked, a concerned look on her face.

"He just got one of our major stash cribs shut down," Tone said, clearly frustrated. "I'm ready to go out and put an end to all this."

"No," Serena said quickly. "You have to stay out of trouble. We can't afford for you to get no more time."

Tone grabbed Serena by her waist. "You gon' hold me down for the whole bid?"

"No doubt."

"Why? I mean, you've only known me for seven months."

"Because you are the first man I've met that has done everything you said you was going to do. And whenever I'm with you, I always feel loved and safe. Besides, I'm a down-ass chick to the fullest, and I look forward to our future together."

Tone didn't even reply. Instead, he just grabbed Serena and tongued her down as the two headed toward the bedroom.

***

Detective Abraham slammed Derrick's face against the hood of the car.

"Yo, man, what the fuck is you doing?"

"Shut the fuck up!" Detective Abraham growled, slapping the handcuffs on him.

"I didn't even do shit!"

"You two weeks late on your taxes," Detective Abraham reminded him. Since his spots had been being robbed lately, he wasn't taking no shit out on the streets. "Either you give me something now, or you go to jail."

"Okay, okay. I got seven grand at the crib. It's yours. Cops ain't supposed to be doing shit like—"

"I ain't no muthafuckin' cop." Detective Abraham caught Derrick off guard with a punch to the stomach, causing him to drop to one knee, doubled over in pain.

"I'm a businessman. One of my men will be by later on to collect that," he said, uncuffing Derrick.

Detective Abraham smirked as he walked back over to his car. Now that one of his main stash houses was shut down, he decided to raise the taxes on the streets. Any hustler that didn't want to get locked up had to pay up. He arrested anybody who didn't pay up then had Maine put their own workers on the block.

The stripper noticed her man's glass was empty. "You need another drink, daddy?"

"Yeah, I'll take another one." Ice-T slapped the stripper's ass as she walked away.

Ice-T was a born hustler, who ran a smooth drug operation and didn't take no shit. Though laid-back, he was deadly. Before he had paid killers on his team, he used to love to put in work. Everybody called him Ice-T because he favored the old-school rapper.

The stripper returned with his drink, and he gladly accepted it. Ice-T watched the sexy woman melt down to her knees in between his legs and begin to suck his dick.

Just as he was getting into it, he saw a cop come up to the front of his house on his surveillance camera. "Hold on, ma," he said, looking hard at the monitors.

"What's wrong?" the stripper asked, wiping her mouth.

"I ain't expecting no company." He stood up and pulled his pants back up, walked over to his closet, and grabbed his MAC-11.

Once Ice-T saw who was coming to his home, he placed his MAC-11 on the coffee table. "Go in the room for a second, baby," he told the stripper as he got up to answer the door.

"How can I help you?"

Detective Abraham smirked. "May I come inside?"

Ice-T sighed loudly as he stepped to the side so the detective could enter.

"You don't look too happy to see me," Detective Abraham said, helping himself to a seat.

"What do you want?" Ice-T said, not hiding the attitude in his voice. "I'm not scheduled to see you for another two weeks."

"Taxes done went up. They coming down on me, so I gotta come down on you."

"How much?"

"Thirty-five percent."

"Get the fuck outta here!" Ice-T yelled. "That's way too much."

"Listen, you already know the rules—You gotta pay to play."

Ice-T didn't like the way the detective just decided to up his prices like that up out the blue. "I'm saying though, this ain't what we agreed on."

"Be smart," Detective Abraham said as he stood up. "Just give up the money. You already know you gonna make it back."

"I'ma pay up this time," Ice-T said. "But next time we gon' have a problem, especially if it's not even time for me to pay yet."

Ice-T went in the back and returned ten minutes later carrying a book bag. "Here take this and get the fuck out!" he said, tossing the book bag at the detective.

"Nice doing business with you." Detective Abraham smiled as he turned and made his exit.

The stripper came back as soon as she heard the door shut. "Everything all right, daddy?" she asked, rubbing Ice-T's shoulders.

Ice-T was watching the detective pull off with his money. "Man, I swear I'm gonna kill that fuckin' cop one of these days."

Serena sat on the couch in the living room getting her relax on. She was holding a glass of red wine and enjoying the sounds of Mary J. Blige that flowed softly through the speakers, when a loud knock at the door startled her, causing her to flinch.

"Who is it?" she yelled, walking toward the door. When she reached the door, she quickly looked through the peephole. Malcolm stood on the other side of the door looking extra filthy and stink. She took a deep breath before opening the door. "Hey. How you do-ing?" she asked in a polite voice.

"Hey. How you doing?" Malcolm said, crust all in his voice. "Is my brother home?"

"No, he's not here right now."

"Oh, okay. Can you please tell him I stopped by?" Malcolm turned to leave.

Serena stopped him. "Hold on. Are you hungry?"

"Starving."

"Come on in. I'll make you something to eat."

Serena pulled out her cell phone and dialed Tone's number. He finally answered on the fifth ring.

"Hey, baby. What's up?"

"Your brother just stopped by here looking for you. Is it okay if I make him something to eat?"

"Yeah, that's cool. Hook him up. I should be there in about an hour, a'ight."

"No problem, baby. See you soon." Serena headed to the kitchen. "What would you like to eat?"

"It doesn't matter," Malcolm answered quickly. "Beggars can't be choosy." He smiled.

"How about some fried chicken and macaroni and cheese?"

Malcolm flashed his fucked-up smile again. "Sounds good to me."

"Coming right up," Serena sang as she poured herself another glass of red wine.

"So how did you and my brother hook up?"

"I don't know," Serena answered with a smile. "It kind of just happened." Just the mention of Tone's name brought a smile to her face.

"I know my brother can be a handful sometimes, but trust me, he's a good guy," Malcolm assured her. "He even saved my life once or twice."

"And I'm pretty sure you've saved his life once or twice as well."

"Have you ever met our father?"

"Not yet," Serena answered, her back turned as she seasoned the meat.

"He's a real piece of shit."

"Awww, don't say that."

"That piece of shit tried to get me killed—his own son—over two hundred dollars. Can you believe that shit?"

"Everybody makes mistakes," Serena said nicely. She really wanted to tell him to shut the fuck up. "Ummm, you want to get upstairs and take a shower and freshen up before you eat?"

"Do you mind?"

"Not at all," Serena told him. "There's fresh towels in the bathroom, and I'll grab you one of Tone's outfits to put on." She escorted Malcolm up to the bathroom.

"Thank you so much. I appreciate it." Malcolm entered the bathroom and shut the door behind him. Serena picked out a nice outfit for him and laid it across the bed as she went back downstairs to finish cooking. Ten minutes later Tone walked through the front door. "Hey, baby. What's up? My brother still here?"

"Yeah, he's upstairs taking a shower. I hope you don't mind, but I laid out one of your outfits for him to put on."

"Nah, it's all good. How he looking?"

"Still the same," Serena said, as nice as possible.

Tone shook his head. "He ain't gon' never be able to get off that pipe."

"He will, baby. It just takes time."

"What takes time?" Malcolm asked, walking down the steps.

Tone yelled, "You getting off that shit! How long is this shit gonna take?"

Malcolm smirked. "How dare you talk to me like that?" he said, walking up on his little brother. "Last I remember, Pops was trying to get you to get high, and I stepped in and took on the drugs so you wouldn't have to. But now you talk to me like I'm an animal?"

"Trying a drug doesn't turn you into a fiend," Tone said.

Malcolm smiled. "Thank you for the clothes, Serena." He walked toward the door.

"What about your food?" she called out.

"I'm not even hungry anymore," Malcolm said as he walked out the door.

Once Serena was sure he was gone, she said, "You didn't have to talk to him like that."

"Fuck him! Muthafucka needs to start taking better care of himself, plain and simple."

"What was he talking about when he said he took on the drugs so you wouldn't have to?"

"I don't know," Tone lied. "The nigga was probably high." He knew exactly what Malcolm was talking about.

Serena laughed. "For real, baby, what was he talking about?"

"Back in the day my pops was always complaining about how his job never paid him enough money. That's the reason Mom left him. From then on, he decided he was going to take his money and that we was going to help him."

Tone's mind drifted back to a few years earlier.

"Get over here," Detective Abraham huffed as he shoved Tone over toward the kitchen. "What's that?" he asked, pointing at the drugs on the kitchen table.

"Drugs," Tone answered nervously.

Detective Abraham tested him, "What kind of drugs?"

"Umm, cocaine?" Tone guessed. Being only seventeen, all he knew was, it was white and it was drugs.

"What makes you think this is cocaine?"

"Because it's white."

"Listen, Tone," Detective Abraham began, "the only way you will ever know what you working with is by tasting it." He scooted the plate over toward Tone.

Tone stuck his finger in the powdered substance and put it in his mouth like he'd seen his father and Malcolm do so many times.

"I mean, you got to taste it."

Tone looked up at his father, before bending down to pick up the small cut-up piece of straw.

Just as he was about to take a snort, Malcolm stepped in. "Fuck is you doing?" he barked.

"Mind your business," Detective Abraham said sternly. "The boy gotta always taste his product."

Malcolm saw the nervous and scared look on Tone's face and knew he had to think quick. "Gimme. I'll taste it."

"No, I told Anthony to taste it."

"I'm the oldest, so I'll taste it." Malcolm took the straw from Tone's hand and sniffed the product.

Malcolm looked over at Tone when he was finished, and Tone silently mouthed the words "Thank you."

From there on out, Malcolm decided to keep on sniffing the drug, until that high wasn't enough.

"And that's how it started."

"That's horrible." Serena exhaled loudly. "Who would do something like that to their own child?"

Tone just smirked. "And ever since then he's been hooked on drugs. He started out just sniffing here and there, and then the shit just got out of hand. The nigga started stealing and everything."

"For real?"

"Yup, my pops even pistol-whipped him and made him strip butt naked in front of everybody. But fuck all that, baby. It is what it is." Tone bent down and kissed Serena on the lips. "I just came to grab something real quick. I gotta head out for a minute with Maine. I love you," Tone said as he flew out the door. "I'll call you later."

Serena watched Tone back out of the driveway. "Be careful out there, baby!" she yelled.

***

Tone pulled up in front of the strip club and quickly spotted Maine and Young Mike standing out front. "What's good, li'l niggas?"

"Li'l niggas?" Maine echoed. "Nigga, please. I'ma *O.G.* out this muthafucka."

"Let me go park this bitch real quick."

Tone swerved into a parking spot and walked back to the front of the club, and the three men entered. Once inside the trio chose a small area over in the corner.

"Bring us one bottle of champagne and a bottle of red wine, please," Tone told the waitress.

"So you ready to do this time?" Maine joked.

"Hell, fuck no," Tone said, shaking his head. "Them five years gon' take forever to go by."

"Just try to keep yourself busy," Young Mike said, as if it was just that easy.

"Nigga, it ain't shit to do in jail," Tone said, and him and Maine burst out laughing. "Speaking of jail, what's up with them fools, Harlem and Smith?"

"Harlem about to be released within the next week 'cause he's a minor," Young Mike replied.

"Damn! He getting off scot-free?" Maine asked, his face crumpled up.

"Nah, five years probation," Young Mike told him.

Tone asked, "What about Smith?"

"Looking like he gon' have to sit for about three years."

"Damn!" Maine banged his fist on the table. "If that nigga didn't freeze up, he would've got away. Shit, as soon as I saw them flashing lights in my mirror, I was out."

"Well, he got three years to learn from his mistake," Tone said.

Just then the waitress returned carrying their bottles.

"Look at this clown," Maine said, staring at the club's entrance. "I'm just waiting for a reason to smoke this nigga."

"Who?"

Tone and Young Mike both turned around to see Ice-T entering the strip club looking like new money. Behind him was Nut, his number one shooter. Nut stood at about five foot eleven inches and weighed about 160 pounds, but whatever his body lacked, his heart made up for it. Following Nut was several youngblood niggas, all dying to prove themselves to him. If anything popped off, they were definitely going to turn it up in the club without thinking twice.

"Them niggas ain't bothering nobody." Tone waved over a thick dark-skinned stripper.

The stripper walked up to Tone. "Hey, daddy," she whispered in his ear, mushing his face into her titties.

"Let me see what you working with," Tone said as he slapped her ass.

The stripper then turned and bent over, spreading her ass cheeks open in Tone's face. "You like that, don't you, daddy?" She started making her ass clap in Tone's face.

"Damn!" Tone said out loud. He sprinkled a few singles on the stripper's back.

Nut had noticed Maine looking at them for the past twenty minutes and didn't like it one bit. "Yo, if this nigga look over here one more time, I'm popping off."

"Who that?" Ice-T asked, looking through his dark-tinted shades. "That's Tone and his crew, right?"

"Yeah," Nut answered, not really caring for Tone either.

Ice-T sat back and pulled a stripper down onto his lap, and she started playing with his ponytail. No mat-

ter where he went, he always sported a ponytail and
dark shades.

"Tone is cool," Ice-T said. "I don't know about the
rest of them niggas. Matter of fact, tell the waitress to
send a bottle to their table on me."

"What the fuck is this?" Maine asked as the waitress
sat a bottle of champagne on their table.

"Paid for by the gentleman over there," the waitress
said, pointing over toward Ice-T's table.

Maine huffed, "We don't want that shit. Go take that
shit back and tell him I said he can shove that bottle up
his ass!"

Tone and Young Mike was so busy being entertained
by sexy dancers, they hadn't even seen the waitress ap-
proach their table.

"Hey, that guy over there refused to take the bottle
and told me to tell you to shove it up your ass, sir," the
waitress reported.

A smirk danced on Ice-T's lips as he stood up and
headed over toward Tone's table, with Nut and the
thirsty youngblood niggas on his heels.

"Yo, we got company," Young Mike said, tapping
Tone's leg as he saw Ice-T and his crew approaching.

Ice-T stopped directly in front of Maine. "You got a
problem over here, fam?"

"You want a problem over here?" Maine shot back.

Tone stepped in between the two. "Yo, what's good?"

"Ya man over here acting like he want a problem.
I tried to send y'all a bottle over here, and he talking
about, shove it up my ass." Ice-T never took his eyes off
Maine. "You need to control that nigga."

Maine looked at Ice-T like he was insane. "Control
me?"

With the quickness of a cat, Maine swung around Tone and punched Ice-T in his face. Then Nut punched Maine in his face.

Next thing you know, all hell broke loose, with fists swinging from every direction in an all-out brawl, sending strippers running to get out of harm's way.

The bouncers finally ran and tried to separate the two crews. All Tone could remember was being choked by a bouncer then being maced, followed by being tossed outside on the curb. Tone stood up and saw police everywhere.

"Let's go, sir." An officer pushed Tone toward the parking lot. "Either go home, or go to jail," he yelled.

Tone made sure he spotted Maine and Young Mike first before he limped over toward his car. "Fuck them niggas!" he said to himself, waving them off as he slid in his car. He looked in the rearview mirror, trying to see how much damage had been done to his face. *Bitch-ass niggas!* He made his car come to life with a turn of the key.

As soon as Tone stepped inside the house, he noticed that Serena was in the kitchen making herself a sandwich.

"Hey, baby. You hungry?" She quickly noticed his busted lip and a few scratches on his face. "What happened to your face?"

Tone sat down at the kitchen table. "I got into a fight at the strip club."

"You better not had been in there fighting over none of them bitches, or else I'ma kick your ass myself," Serena said as she walked off to go get the alcohol and some tissue.

"The only bitch you'll ever catch me fighting over is you. But fuck all that! We need to figure out how we gon' keep this money pouring in while I'm locked up."

"I'm all ears," Serena said as she cleaned Tone's wounds.

"A'ight. Well, this how we gon' do this. After you get the work, all you gotta do is drop it off to Maine, and he'll handle everything else. All you gotta do is sit back and collect the money."

"How much will he be giving me?"

"He'll be giving you all the re-up money and our profit."

"You sure he can be trusted? 'Cause that's a lot of money."

"Most definitely. I'd put my life on it."

"That's all I needed to hear." Serena smiled as she kissed Tone's busted lip.

"You just make sure you handle your business."

"You ain't gotta worry about me. My business gonna get handled and handled well, might I add," Serena said, her hands on her hips.

Tone looked down at Serena's sexy-ass legs and pedicured toes, and his dick immediately got hard. "Why don't you handle your business right now?" he said as he pulled out his dick.

The words barely left his mouth before Serena was all over him. She slowly began kissing on his inner thighs then played with the head with the tip of her tongue, before taking him all the way in her mouth.

Serena had Tone moaning loudly, letting warm saliva run down the shaft and over her hand. Skillfully she tried to relax the muscles in her throat and deep-throated as much as she could. She tried her hardest not to gag and take the dick like a pro. But she couldn't, not with Tone fucking her mouth like he hated her.

"Ooh shit, baby," he groaned. "Ya daddy about to come. You ready for it?"

"Um-hmm." Serena started sucking even harder.

With a grunt, Tone's body went stiff as he exploded in her mouth. "Well, damn!" he said, out of breath.

"Don't test my skills ever again." Serena smiled as she grabbed her sandwich off the counter and headed to the bedroom.

Chapter 13

Gruff pulled over and double-parked behind a van. "How your ribs feeling?"

"They a'ight," Maxine replied, still in pain.

"A'ight, cool. I want you to wait here." Gruff slid out the car and walked up to this young kid who was outside slanging. "Yo, what's good?" he asked the young man. "Can I get six for fifty-five?"

"Yeah, I got you," the young'un answered, looking over both shoulders.

"A'ight, we gotta do this in the building," Gruff said. "It's too many people out here." He walked off in the direction of the building, looking over his shoulder. He grinned when he saw the young hustler following behind him.

Gruff snatched the young hustler into the staircase as soon as he entered the building. "Get over here, you little muthafucka!" he growled. He quickly stuck his 9 mm up under the kid's chin. "I need to fine Tone."

"I don't know nobody named Tone," the young hustler said, scared to death.

"Well, li'l nigga, you better tell me something, and you got to the count of three. Two—"

"Okay, okay," the young hustler said, pleading for his life. "All I know is that there's a new main stash house out in Brooklyn."

"Where at in Brooklyn?" Gruff asked through clenched teeth.

"In Flatbush. I got a pen in my pocket. I'll write down the address for you."

"You better not be lying, li'l nigga. That's all I'ma tell you."

The look on Gruff's face said it all.

"I'm not lying." The young hustler handed Gruff the piece of paper with the address of the new stash house on it.

Gruff took all the money and work the young hustler had on him. "Get the fuck outta here!" he said, dismissing the young street punk. "I catch you out here again and I'ma clap you. You too fuckin' young to be out here any damn way." Gruff grumbled all the way back to the car.

"Did you get that nigga's address?" Maxine asked, a thirsty look on her face.

Gruff flashed a rare smile. "Even better. I got the address to them niggas' new stash crib."

"Let's do it." Maxine was ready to get some payback on the crew that had shot her. "I'm tired of playing with these bitches. We fixin' to turn it all the way up out here on these streets!"

Ice-T looked inside the book bag of cash. "Damn! This shit looking kinda short."

"Nah, Greg said it was all there," Nut said, slowing down for the yellow light. "If that shit is short, then just let me know, and I'll go handle that."

"Oh shit!" Ice-T spotted Tone coming out of IHOP with a woman by his side. "There go that nigga Tone right there. Pull over."

Nut quickly pulled up, stopped directly in front of the couple, and whipped out his .45.

"Nah, chill," Ice-T said. "I just want to talk to him." He slid out the passenger seat. "Stay in the car."

As Tone and Serena walked up out of IHOP, he saw a car make a sharp stop in front of them. Immediately his hand gripped the handle of his .40-cal. He saw Ice-T getting out of the passenger seat.

"Baby, go wait for me in the car," Tone said, never taking his eyes off of Ice-T. Once Ice-T was close enough, Tone said, "What's good?"

"I just want to talk," Ice-T said, sticking both hands down into his pocket. "My bad about the other night. I didn't want it to go down like that."

"Yeah, me either. But, hey, shit happens."

"What's up with ya man, though?" Ice-T asked.

"Who Maine?"

"Yeah. What's his problem? I ain't never did nothing to that brother for him to be acting like that."

"He just be buggin' sometimes."

"Well, I know that's ya man and everything. That's why I wanted to talk to you." Ice-T looked over both shoulders before adding, "I need you to calm that fool down, before I have him killed."

"Listen, Maine is like a brother to me—"

"I already know where you going with this," Ice-T said, cutting Tone off mid-sentence. "I'm going to stay out of his way. I just hope he does the same."

Tone nodded his head. "That's fair enough."

"Heard you gotta go do a little time in a few days."

"Yeah, I'm just ready to go in and get this shit over with." Tone noticed the nasty look Nut was giving him from the car.

"You need anything, you know how to get in contact with me." Ice-T gave Tone a pound and headed back to his ride.

"I don't know why you wasting your time talking to that clown," Nut said. "His pops is the one extorting us."

"Tone is cool," Ice-T said. "It's the rest of them fools on his team that I can't stand."

"So what you want us to do if we run across that nigga Maine again?" Nut asked, his eyes on the road.

"We bump into him again," Ice-T said, thumbing through the cash in the book bag again, "and he act like he want it, we gon' give it to him."

Nut smiled. "Say no more."

"Is everything all right?" Serena asked when Tone got to the car.

"Yeah, everything is straight," Tone answered quickly. He respected Ice-T, and was hoping things didn't get out of hand with the two crews again, 'cause the next time someone was sure to get killed.

"Baby, can I ask you something?"

"Yeah. What's up?"

"When you go away to do this time, ain't nobody gonna be trying to kill me, trying to get to you, are they?" Serena asked seriously.

Tone chuckled. "Nah, baby. You gon' be straight. The most a nigga might try to do is get my pussy."

"Well, you know that shit ain't gonna never fuckin' happen," Serena said in a matter-of-fact tone.

"I look worried to you?" Tone asked with a smirk. He trusted Serena and was glad to have her on his team. He was just ready to go in and get his time started. The sooner he went in, the sooner he would get out.

"You better not be worried." Serena said it like she was gonna slap him.

Tone answered his ringing cell phone as he slowed down for the red light. "Yeah, what's up?" he answered.

"Get to the stash house right this minute." *Click!*

Tone hung up the phone and made a quick detour. He didn't recognize the number, but he definitely recognized his father's voice.

"Where we going?" Serena asked.

"Gotta make a quick stop."

By the look on Tone's face, Serena could tell that something was up, but she just sat back and kept quiet.

Ten minutes later Tone pulled up in front of a regular-looking house and placed the car in park. "Wait right here, baby. I'll be back in a second."

Tone stepped foot inside the house and immediately covered his nose. "What the fuck is going on in here?"

"This is some bullshit, that's what's going on around here," Detective Abraham said, pointing at all the dead bodies laying around.

Tone looked around and saw about twelve men who looked like they had been eaten by some kind of animal or something. "Who the fuck did this shit?"

"That bitch-ass nigga, Gruff." Maine remembered that Monique's body looked the same way when he had found her. "He let his punk-ass dog eat 'em up."

"Fuck!" Detective Abraham said loudly. "This the second major stash crib in a month. How the fuck does this nigga know where we operate at?"

"Nigga must got a inside plug," Tone said, looking at all the chewed-up dead bodies laying around. "Whoever it is, we need to find him and soon!"

"Fuck it! From now on, only us three will know where the stash cribs are," Detective Abraham said. "Well, you'll be in jail in the next forty-eight hours, so I guess just me and you will know the locations," he said, looking over at Maine.

"I don't understand how nobody don't know where this fool live at," Maine huffed. "Wherever I bump into that nigga at, it's going down. One of us is gonna get killed, either him or me."

"Chill. You wildin'," Tone said, laughing at Maine's last comment.

"So what's good, son?" Detective Abraham asked. "When you go to do your time, this bitch still gonna be getting the work for us, right?"

"Yeah, I got everything set up already, and don't call her a bitch" Tone said checking his pops.

"Oooh shit! Excuseeee me," Detective Abraham said, and him and Maine busted out laughing. "Let me find out shorty got you all falling in love and shit."

Tone shook his head. "Maybe if y'all got y'all some business, y'all wouldn't always have to be all in mines."

"You know we just playing," Maine said, throwing two phantom punches at Tone. "If you feeling shorty, then do what you gotta do."

"I *am* feeling her, more than I planned on, too," Tone told them. "It's like she's perfect for me. I know it started out as a scam we was running, but she is a real good woman."

"Well, you know they say everything happens for a reason, so if she makes you happy then I'm cool with it." Maine gave Tone a pound followed by a hug.

"I'ma need you to look out for her while I'm away," Tone told him.

"Whatever you need, you know I got you."

"Just make sure nobody ain't trying to rob her or no dumb shit," Tone said.

"I got you."

"A'ight. I'ma holla at y'all before I turn myself in," Tone said as he exited the stash house.

Once Tone was out of the house, Detective Abraham, a look of disgust on his face, huffed, "Pussy-whipped muthafucka! I could've sworn I taught that fool better than that."

When Tone got back in the car, Serena asked, "Everything okay, baby?"

"Yeah, everything is cool," Tone said as he pulled off. "I'ma drop you off at the crib then I'ma go holla at Young Mike for a minute. I won't be long no longer than an hour."

"No problem, baby. Handle your business."

Twenty minutes later Tone pulled up in front of his house and let Serena out. "I'll be back in about an hour, a'ight."

"Okay, baby," Serena said as she leaned in for a kiss.

Tone stepped foot inside the bar and quickly spotted Young Mike over at the bar trying to holla at a nice li'l light-skin thing. He needed to holla at Young Mike, and he also needed a drink.

"What's good, my nigga?" Tone said, interrupting Young Mike's conversation.

"Ma, I'ma holla at you later, a'ight," Young Mike said to the chick. "What's popping, my nigga?" He turned and gave Tone a pound.

"You know I turn myself in the day after tomorrow. I just need you to look after Serena for me while I'm away."

"A'ight. What you need me to do?" Young Mike asked.

"Just make sure she getting the proper money that she's supposed to."

"You know I got you," Young Mike said, giving Tone a pound.

As the two sat at the bar talking and having drinks, Gruff and Maxine walked up in the joint.

"I need a muthafuckin' drink," Maxine said, her and Gruff walking right past Tone and Young Mike.

"You a alcoholic," Gruff said as the two sat over in the corner.

"Remind me to buy Tiger a big-ass steak," Maxine said, "because she been putting in some real work."

"That's what she's supposed to do. She was the only family I ever had until I met you, and I'm the only family she got as well."

"Aww, ain't that sweet," Maxine teased, but Gruff didn't laugh. Instead, his focus was over at the bar.

"What happen?" Maxine asked, following Gruff's eyes.

Gruff had to do a double take just to make sure his eyes weren't playing tricks on him. "There go that bitch-ass nigga Tone right there." He smiled.

Maxine, ready to put in some work, pulled out her .357. "Where?"

"Right over there," Gruff said, holding Maxine's shooting hand with one and pointing with the other.

"Want me to run over there and push his shit back?"

Gruff told her, "Nah, we gon' catch him outside."

"Let's do this nigga right now," Maxine pressed. "This nigga don't even know what we look like."

"Too many witnesses in here," Gruff said, looking around. "Plus, we been dropping mad bodies. God forbid, we get caught, them crackers gon' try to make an example out of us."

Maxine sucked her teeth, but she knew what Gruff was saying was the truth. "I don't care how we do it, as long as it gets done."

"Shit. That nigga should be thanking us, 'cause we doing him a favor." Gruff downed another shot. "I know I'll rather get killed than go back to jail."

Maxine gave him dap. "I know that's right."

Gruff stood up. "Come on, let's go outside and wait for this clown." On the way out he tossed his hood over his head and walked right past Tone and Young Mike the same way he had walked in.

***

"What you getting into when you leave here?" Young Mike asked.

"I'm gonna go home and fuck my girl until it's time for me to go to jail." Tone laughed as he stood up and paid the tab.

"If I don't see you before you go in, hold ya head," Young Mike said as he gave Tone a pound and a strong hug.

"That time gon' fly once I get in there." Tone smiled as him and Young Mike exited the bar.

"Yo, you get home safe, a'ight," Tone said as he walked over to his car and slid in the driver's seat. Once he was inside his car, he just sat there for minute just thinking about the decisions he had made in the last six months.

Mya came to his mind. He knew their relationship was over, but he didn't want any hard or negative feelings toward her.

Fuck it! The least I can do is go give her an apology. Tone started the engine and headed for Mya's house.

As soon as Tone pulled out of the parking lot, Maxine slowly cruised out right behind him.

Tone pulled up in front of his old residence and got out the car. He walked up to the door and gave it a medium knock. Mya answered the door, still looking sexy, even with the big bulge in her stomach.

"Hey," Tone said, looking Mya up and down.

"Hey," Mya replied.

"Can I come in? Please, I need to talk to you."

"Nah, I don't think that's a good idea."

"Come on, don't act like that. I just need to talk to you. It'll only take five minutes."

Mya stepped to the side so Tone could enter. "Five minutes is all you get."

"Can I sit down?"

"No, you can stand," Mya said, her arms folded across her chest.

"I just came over here to apologize about how we ended. You was nothing but good to me, and I took you for granted. I just wanted to say sorry, and I hope we can still be friends and hope you will allow me to see my baby."

"Well, you should be sorry. I was ready to marry you and be your wife and the mother of your child, and you threw all that away for some stupid money." Mya's eyes began to water. "And you didn't have to do it 'cause we already had enough money to last us almost a lifetime."

Tone said quickly, "Four hundred thousand ain't lasting no lifetime."

"You see, that's all you care about is money—money this, and money that. Well, you can take all that money and shove it up your ass!" she yelled, tears streaming down.

"Listen, I just came over here to tell you I was sorry. I didn't come here for all this."

Just then they heard a knock at the door. Mya walked over to the door, looked through the peephole, then quickly opened it. In stepped the guy who was in the house the last time Tone was there, the one who was wearing the suit.

"Hey, baby. How you doing?" He leaned down and kissed Mya on the cheek. "These are for you," he said, removing a dozen red roses from behind his back.

"Awwww, thank you, Russel," Mya said as she gave him a hug.

Russel was about to say something, until he spotted Tone standing in the living room. Mya then introduced the two. "Russel, this is Tone. Tone, this is Russel."

"Nice to meet you, brother," Russel said, extending his hand.

Tone looked at Russel's hand like it was infected then looked back at Mya. "I'ma holla at you later. I just came by to say sorry." Tone walked right past Russel's extended hand as he headed for the door.

"How rude," Russel said in a proper tone.

Tone thought about turning around and smacking the shit outta that clown, but instead just decided to leave. "I'll holla at you later." He opened up the door and stepped outside and saw two figures jogging in his direction. Immediately he stepped back inside the house, slammed the door, and tackled Mya to the floor.

"Hey, what do you think you're doing?" Russel said. "I'm calling 9-1-1."

Before Russel could even reach the phone a loud series of gunshots hit the front door, blowing big chunks of wood from off the door.

Tone pulled out his .45 and quickly escorted Mya into the kitchen. "Here, stay down behind this counter." He saw Russel running upstairs like a scared little bitch.

Gruff aimed his Uzi at the front lock, shot it off, then kicked open the front door. He stepped inside, slowly looking around, with a two-handed grip on his weapon. His eyes quickly turned toward the kitchen when he heard somebody sniffing like they was crying.

Tone quickly sprung up from behind the counter firing. *BOOM! BOOM! BOOM! BOOM!*

Gruff quickly ran around the corner and got low. He looked over at the door and gave Maxine hand signals to exactly where Tone was hiding.

"I see you, muthafucka!" Tone yelled as he sent two shots toward the front door, backing Maxine up.

Gruff popped up from around the corner and did an army roll as he squeezed the trigger on his Uzi. Tone

ducked down just in time as him and Mya watched bulletholes rip through the refrigerator.

"Stop hiding, you little bitch!" Gruff yelled as he gave
Maxine some more hand signals.

Upstairs, Russel grabbed the cordless phone off the
charger and quickly dialed 9-1-1.

"Stay right here and don't move," Tone whispered to
Mya. He was praying nothing happened to their child
that she was carrying.

Gruff emptied his whole clip on the counter, hoping
a few bullets might've penetrated. "We gotta go!" He
grabbed Maxine, and the two fled from the scene.

"Are they gone?" Mya asked with a scared-to-death
look in her eyes.

Tone jumped up from behind the counter, holding
his gun sideways. He quickly scanned the place. "Yeah,
it looks like they gone." He helped Mya to her feet. "I
need a favor," he said, holding out the gun. "I gotta get
outta here before the cops get here!"

Mya looked at the gun for a second before she took
it. "Go. Get outta here before you get caught." She lifted
up the cage on the top of the stove and sat the gun
down before closing it back, like Tone had taught her a
long time ago.

"And don't worry about the house," Tone yelled over
his shoulder as he ran up out the house. "I'll take care
of it."

"Baby, you okay?" Russel yelled from upstairs.

"Yeah, I'm fine. Get down here."

"Oh my God!" he said, looking at all the bulletholes
everywhere. "I don't think you should let him back
in your house again." Russel heard the sirens getting
louder. "I think we should press charges when the cops
get here."

"When the cops get here, I need you to just be quiet.
We didn't see nothing, and we don't know nothing,"
Mya said, already knowing the drill.

With a raised eyebrow, Russel asked, "You sure you want to do that?"

"Positive," Mya said sternly. "When they ask, we gon' say somebody just shot up our house and we ran for cover upstairs and didn't see nobody faces, okay?"

"I guess." Russel couldn't understand why Mya didn't want to tell the police what really happened.

"Yo, pass that Dutch, nigga." Maine snatched it from the hands of a young hustler. "Damn! You got the shit all wet and shit," he complained as him, Young Mike, and a few other hustlers on the team stood in front of the building getting high, getting their drink on, and talking shit.

"Shit, all these li'l niggas just hanging around and shit," Maine huffed. "Y'all niggas 'bout to have to start putting in work out here on these streets."

Right on cue, a tall guy walked up with a hard jail-house bop and a mean look on his face. Maine stepped in the tall man's path. "Yo, fam, who you coming to see in this hood?"

"What?" the tall guy said, his face in a frown.

Before he could even say another word, he felt a punch to the back of his head followed by a bottle being shattered over his head. The tall man hit the ground and felt hands and feet coming from all directions.

"That's enough," Maine yelled, and him and his crew watched the tall man stagger back up to his feet, all bloody. Maine wagged his finger. "Don't come up in this hood again!"

Young Mike just sat over to the side sipping from his white foam cup, shaking his head. "Y'all niggas is mad dumb."

Maine turned to face Young Mike. "Fuck is you talking about?"

"What if that nigga come back blasting?"

"What? You scared or something?"

Maine and the rest of the crew busted out laughing.

"Scared?" Young Mike echoed looking at Maine like he was crazy. "If he come back blasting, that's not good for business. You must've forgot—We in this for the money, not a rep."

Maine stepped to Young Mike. "Yo, you got a problem with how I'm running shit?"

"Last I heard, Tone was still in charge," Young Mike shot back.

"Tone goes to turn himself in tomorrow for five years," Maine reminded him. "So therefore I'm in charge," he said, pounding on his chest.

"Like I said, last I heard, Tone was still in charge. Until I hear otherwise, that's what it is." Young Mike took another sip from his foam cup.

Maine was just about to steal on Young Mike, until one of the young hustlers yelled, "Damn! She got a fat ass!"

Maine looked in the other direction and saw a thick chocolate thing dressed half-naked headed toward the building they was standing in front of. From the looks of it, he could tell that she was just coming from the club.

"Damn, ma! Where the party at?" Maine grabbed the woman's arm, stopping her in mid-stride.

"What is you doing?" the woman yelled. She jerked her arm out of Maine's grip. "Don't put ya fuckin' hands on me! Fuckin' bum-ass niggas!"

"Bitch, who the fuck you talking to like that?"

"Nigga, I'm talking to you." The woman looked Maine up and down, a look of disgust on her face. "Y'all muthafuckas don't know how to talk to a real woman. That's why y'all gon' always be standing in front of this building looking stupid."

Just as she got ready to walk in the building, Maine snuffed her from behind, knocking her the fuck out.

The whole crew bust out, "Ooooooohhhh!"

"Fuck is you doing?" Young Mike asked, shaking his head, helping the young lady get back to her feet.

"Look at this sucker-for-love-ass nigga." Maine laughed, pointing at Young Mike.

"What you just call me?" Young Mike asked, dropping the woman back down to the ground. "You disrespecting me?"

"Yeah. Fuck you gon' do about it?"

Before Young Mike could reply, a younger hustler quickly jumped in front of him, so the two men wouldn't clash.

"You a bitch-ass nigga!" Young Mike said as he walked off. He wanted to pull out his ratchet and pop Maine's head off right in front of the building, but he couldn't afford to fuck up his money.

Maine yelled at Young Mike's back, "Yeah, you better walk the fuck off!" He watched the woman get up and stumble in the building. "Tired of these young niggas out here running they fuckin' mouth. Next nigga say some wild shit, I'm popping the fuck off."

"I'm going to get my brother," the woman said, as she disappeared inside the building.

"I told you we should've got that nigga Tone when we had the chance," Maxine said, pulling up in front of the weed spot.

Gruff rolled down the window and called the young kid over. "Yo, shorty, lemme get five twenties." He pulled out a big wad of cash.

The young kid pulled the weed from out of his pocket and stood there.

"Nigga, lemme see how big them shits is," Gruff said with an attitude.

The young kid thought about it for a second then dropped the bags of weed in Gruff's hand.

"Damn! These shits look like you been tapping the bags," Gruff said with a smirk on his face.

Right after he said that, Maxine stepped on the gas, leaving the young kid standing there, looking stupid.

"Dumb-ass kids." Gruff shook his head. "Selling drugs ain't for everybody."

"I know that's right," Maxine said. "What's our next move?"

"We gon' lay low for a hot minute and let the heat on the streets die down," Gruff replied. "It's mad hot, and the streets is talking right now."

"Damn! So what the fuck am I supposed to do while this heat is dying down?"

"Whatever the fuck you wanna do." Gruff shrugged his shoulders. "I think I'ma go to Atlantic City for a month and cool out."

"Atlantic City?" Maxine repeated. "What the fuck is out there?"

"A peace of mind," Gruff answered quickly. "You should roll."

"Nah, I'm good," Maxine said, waving off the idea. She pulled up to the sleazy motel they had been staying at for the past few days. "I'll be here when you get back."

Chapter 14

Tone stood in front of the mirror fully dressed, just staring at himself. Today was the day he was going to turn himself in, and suddenly he wasn't in such a rush to get this day started. Several things ran through his mind. He knew for a fact he was going to miss Serena, along with a lot of other things he had to give up.

"You all right, baby?" Serena asked, wrapping her arms around Tone's waist from behind.

Tone turned around, so the two could face each other. "Yeah, I'm cool. I just hate that I gotta be away from you for so damn long sitting up behind a wall."

He huffed as he heard somebody ringing his doorbell. He looked through the peephole and opened the door and walked away from it.

"Good morning to you too," Detective Abraham said with a smile as he stepped inside the house, followed by Maine. "You not gon' introduce me to this young lady I've been hearing so much about?"

"Serena, this my pops," Tone said dryly. "Pops, this is Serena."

Detective Abraham smiled. "How you doing, sweetheart?"

Tone opened up the fridge, pulled out a bottle of Coconut Cîroc, and turned up the bottle. "Fuck!" he said loudly, out of frustration.

"Stop crying," Detective Abraham said. "You acting like you never gonna get out."

"That's not the point." Tone took another sip from the bottle.

"Do you and Maine got this money situation under control?" Detective Abraham asked, a greedy look in his eyes.

"Yeah, everything is already taken care of," Tone assured him. "Come on, let's get this show on the road," he said as he exited his crib.

Tone slid in the driver's seat of his Range Rover.

"You don't want me to drive, baby?" Serena asked, sliding in the passenger seat.

"Nah, I got it." Tone took another swig from his bottle. "This gon' be my last time driving for a while." He smirked as he followed Maine and his father down to the courthouse.

When Tone stopped at a red light, Serena unzipped his pants and pulled out his dick.

"Damn, baby! I don't think my shit work anymore." Tone was still sore from the nonstop sex they'd had all night and morning. "It ain't no more come left in there."

"I'll find some." Serena went straight to work on her man's dick, sucking it like it was so delicious.

Tone stepped inside the courtroom and saw about twenty-five to thirty members from his team in the courtroom supporting him. He looked over to his right and saw Mya sitting over in the corner, her eyes watery. He smoothly gave her a head nod and a wink as he went and stood next to his lawyer.

After about ten minutes of big-time lawyer talk, three officers came and grabbed Tone and escorted him to the back.

Right before he disappeared in the back, Serena yelled, tears running down her face, "I love you, baby, and I'ma be right here waiting for you when you get out. Hold it down!"

Serena hopped back in the Range Rover and started the engine. She was getting ready to pull out of the parking spot, until she saw the other woman who was in the courtroom flagging down her truck.

"Can I help you?" Serena asked politely.

"I just wanted to tell you thanks for fucking up a happy home," Mya said, an evil look on her face.

Serena shot back, "I ain't fuck up shit. Tone told me all about y'all's relationship, and you just need to get over it. He's mine now."

"You can have him. But if you ever hurt him or do him wrong, I'ma see you—"

"That was cute." Serena laughed as she pulled off, leaving Mya standing there.

Nut hopped up out of his bed in a hurry. Not many people knew where he lived, so he knew it could've only been one of two people knocking on his door at eleven in the morning. He snatched open the door. "Fuck is banging on door like they the"—Nut's words got stuck in his throat when he saw his sister's face. "Mary, what the fuck happened to you?"

"Some guy beat my ass 'cause I didn't want to talk to him." Mary started sobbing.

Nut sat down on the couch. "Start from the beginning."

"I was going home from the club when I saw a bunch of guys out standing in front of the building. One was trying to holla, but I ignored him." She paused. "So I kept walking and didn't say nothing. Then the guy grabbed me, so I pulled my arm away, and then he just hit me."

"Who is this guy?" Nut asked, his killer face on.

"I don't know," Mary cried.

"If you seen him again, would you be able to point him out to me?"

"Yeah," Mary answered. "I've seen him around a few times, but he always be with a bunch of niggas every time I see him."

"Let me worry me about all that."

Nut answered his ringing cell phone. "What up? . . . Yeah, a'ight. I'll be there in a minute," he said, ending the call.

Nut told his sister, "I'ma call you later on tonight, and we gon' go out and find this nigga who did this to you, a'ight."

"Okay," Mary said, and she got up and left.

"I'm just letting you know how it works around here," Detective Abraham stated plainly.

Mario wanted to smack the shit out of the detective for trying to extort him. "You asking for a little too much."

"Actually, I'm hooking you up," Detective Abraham told him. "Usually, I charge niggas way more. You gotta pay to play out here."

"I'm saying though"—Mario stood up—"I'm not really with all that extortion shit, smell me?"

"I'm not extorting you," Detective Abraham said, trying to downplay his scheme. "But everybody has to pay taxes." He shrugged his shoulders.

Mario chuckled. "Fuck you and your taxes! You want money from me, then you gon' have to take it in blood."

Detective Abraham raised an eyebrow. "That's how you wanna do this?"

"Yeah, that's exactly how I want to do this. And guess what? If I ever see you again, I'm going to kill you. Stay the fuck away from my area!"

Detective Abraham rose to his feet, with a smile on his face. "You got it, big man," he said, and he exited the restaurant.

"Punk-ass cop." Mario shook his head as he hopped in his whip and broke out.

Mario pulled up in front of Ice-T's crib and let the engine die. "He gonna have to tax me," he mumbled to himself as he walked up to the front door and knocked on it.

Ice-T stepped to the side, so Mario could enter. "What's good, my *G*?"

"Yo, I'm about to bust a cap in this punk-ass policeman!"

"What policeman?"

Mario looked down at the card he had left. "Some clown named Detective Abraham."

"Why? What happen?"

"Nigga trying to extort me. You know I don't even get down like that."

"Calm down. I do business with that clown. I'll talk to him for you, a'ight."

"A'ight. But I'm telling you, if the nigga come at me like that again, it's on!" Mario stormed out of Ice-T's crib.

"Fuck wrong with this greedy-ass cocksucker?" Ice-T said out loud. He picked up his cell phone and dialed Detective Abraham's number.

"What's up?" Detective Abraham answered.

"One of my workers just dropped by my crib, talking about you was trying to lean on him. What's up with that?" Ice-T asked.

"Everyone has to get taxed. You already know how I operate."

"Yeah, but Mario gets his work from me, and you already taxing me. So couldn't you just let me slide? 'Cause that would be kinda like you taxing me twice. Know what I mean?"

"No, I don't know what you mean," Detective Abraham shot back. "I'm a businessman, and I'm just doing my job. Ya man don't wanna pay, then he gon' really have to pay, point-blank," he said, ending the call.

"Muthafucka tryin'a bargain and shit. Fuck outta here!" Detective Abraham looked over at Maine. "As a matter of fact, I think I need you to pay that clown a visit tonight. I'm tired of these niggas acting as if they can just do what the fuck they want."

"What's this clown's résumé?" Maine downed a shot of Henny.

"I got you." Detective Abraham pulled up Mario's rap sheet, along with his address, on his computer. "I want you to make this one messy too."

Maine laughed, leaning back in his chair. "Not a problem."

"You see that nigga?" Nut asked, pulling up in front of a crowd of men standing in front of the building where his sister had been attacked the other day.

"Nah, I don't see him." Mary squinted her eyes, so she could get a better look. "He must not be out here today."

"You sure?"

"Yeah, I'm sure."

"We gon' come back every day 'til we find this muthafucka!" Nut pulled off, mad that the person they was looking for wasn't outside.

Maine crept up along the side of Mario's house with his silenced .380 in his hand. He peeked through the kitchen window and saw him standing in the kitchen with his back turned, talking on the phone. Maine quietly placed his .380 on the window, aimed it at the back of Mario's head, and pulled the trigger.

The gun chirped *Spt!* Then Mario's body suddenly collapsed.

Maine then quickly walked around the house to the front door and shot the lock off. He entered the house and headed straight for Mario's body. Then he stood over him and emptied an entire clip into his already dead body. He then reloaded his clip and emptied it into Mario's lifeless body before making his exit.

Maine slid back in his car and drove off like nothing never even happened. "Bitch-ass nigga," he mumbled, picking up his cell phone and calling Detective Abraham.

"What's up?"

"Done!" Maine said, and he hung up.

Maine turned up his new Lil Wayne mixtape and bumped that shit all the way until he got back to the hood. He pulled up in front of the hood and saw all his people standing in front of the building like they always did. He hopped out his whip so he could join them.

"What's good, my niggas?" he said, giving each man dap. "How it's looking out here?"

A man wearing a do-rag replied, "Slow motion."

"Damn! Ain't no bitches out here or nothing?" Maine cracked open a Dutch Masters.

"Nah." Do-rag looked up and saw a familiar-looking black car. He became suspicious. "Yo, son, this same car been riding through here for about the last three days."

"What black car?" Maine looked up with the quickness and instantly spotted a black car with dark-tinted windows just sitting idly at the curb.

"That black car right there." Do-rag nodded.

"Shit! I hope they strapped." Maine laughed, ready for whatever.

Nut was running out of patience. "You still don't see the nigga?"

"I think that's him right there," Mary said, pointing at Maine.

"Oh shit!"

"You know him or something?"

"Yeah, we had a fight a few weeks ago in the club." Nut grabbed his TEC-9 from off the backseat.

"What you about to do?" Mary asked in a panicky voice.

"Nothing."

Nut quickly stepped out the car, aimed his TEC-9 at the building, and pulled the trigger, swinging his arms back and forth three times, trying to hit every last nigga standing in front of the building. Once he ran out of bullets, he hopped back in the car and pulled off, almost hitting an oncoming car.

Mary screamed, "Oh my God!" when she felt something pierce her thigh. She had ducked down in her seat when she heard the back window rip, but she didn't hear any gunshots.

"Yo, if that car still sitting right there by the time I finish rolling this blunt, I'm airing that shit out!" Maine huffed.

"Yo, they getting out," Do-rag announced.

Maine ducked down when he heard gunshots coming from some kind of machine gun ringing out. He quickly hit the ground when he saw members from his crew dropping like flies. Once the shots finished ringing out, he quickly pulled out his .380 and sent two shots through the passenger door.

Before the car pulled off, Maine quickly hopped up to his feet in a wide-legged stance, his two hands on his gun, and fired off about seven shots. He watched four bullets rip through the back window. As the black car disappeared, he was hoping he'd caught a head or two.

"We just came from Mario's crib, and somebody left that nigga stretched out in the kitchen," a worker reported.

"Get the fuck outta here!" Ice-T said, not believing what he'd just heard. "Say word?"

"Word to everything," the worker said seriously.

"Muthafucka!" Ice-T grabbed his phone and dialed Detective Abraham's number. The detective had just crossed the line, pissing Ice-T off.

"Yeah," he answered in an uninterested tone.

"What the fuck is up?" Ice-T yelled. "I thought we had a deal. How you just gon' go and off my man Mario?"

"He was outta line, so he had to be dealt with."

"Mario was making me a lot of money, and now you just fucked that all up!"

"First of all, watch your fuckin' tone when you speak to me," Detective Abraham began. "Second of all, I don't give a fuck about how you feel about Mario. He wasn't shit but a worker anyway."

"So it's like that?" Ice-T asked.

"Just like that."

"Yeah, a'ight," Ice-T said, ending the call. "Fuck! I can't stand that crooked muthafucka!" He threw his glass up against the wall.

"Get Nut on the phone and tell him I said to get over here right now!" Ice-T ordered. It was time to show Detective Abraham who really ran the streets.

An hour later Nut showed up to Ice-T's crib. "Yo, these niggas gon' have to go!"

"What is you talking about?" Ice-T asked.

"That nigga Maine shot my sister in the fuckin' leg. He gotta go, point-blank."

"Well, today must be your fuckin' lucky day." Ice-T smiled. "They just had Mario killed too."

"You see what I'm talking about?" Nut said, clearly frustrated. "Fuck that! I'm ready to go to war."

"Gather up some goons and take out that punk-ass detective first. Then you can do whatever the fuck you want with Maine." Ice-T was sick of Detective Abraham's shit, and he wasn't just going to sit there and let the man do whatever he wanted, just 'cause he was the police.

"About fuckin' time!" Nut huffed as he exited the house so he could get things in motion.

"Let the games begin," Ice-T said to himself, firing up another blunt.

"I see ain't shit change since I been gone," Harlem said, happy to finally be released from jail.

Young Mike reminded him, "Nigga, you was only gone for six punk-ass months."

"Well, that shit felt like forever." Harlem poured himself a cup of Henny. He was so happy to finally be home, and not having to be told what to do and when to do it no more. "So have them stickup kids been back around since I clapped one of 'em up?"

"Yeah, like once or twice, but they been kinda quiet lately." Young Mike was hoping they got the message and didn't come back again. "I don't know what the fuck they up to."

"They must've heard I'm out now," Harlem said, and the two busted out laughing.

"Nah, but I don't know what's up with them fools. They probably got locked up." Just then, Young Mike noticed Maine walking in their direction.

"What's good, li'l niggas?" Maine said, giving both men dap. "What's good for tonight?"

Young Mike still wasn't feeling Maine after how the two men had gotten into it. "Shit, we just chilling, getting our sip on."

"Fuck that! Let's get into something tonight," Maine said excitedly.

"Nah, I just came home today," Harlem told him. "I'ma just chill for the night."

"Y'all niggas always acting like some bitches!" Maine walked off mad 'cause Harlem and Young Mike just wanted to chill in the hood for the night.

"Somebody gon' kill that nigga one of these days." Young Mike shook his head at how ignorant Maine could be at times for no reason.

"Li'l bitch-ass niggas," Maine huffed as he slid in his Yukon.

With nothing else to do, Maine decided to go to a strip club and enjoy himself. He pulled up across the street from the strip club and let the engine die. Before he got out the truck, he put the money he planned on spending aside from his regular money.

Maine walked up to the front door and was immediately patted down.

"Fam, you can't come in here with that!" the bouncer said, nodding toward the gun in his waist.

"Come on, son, I ain't gon' shoot nobody," Maine pleaded.

"Doesn't matter," the bouncer said, shaking his head no. "No hammers allowed inside."

"Fuck!" Maine cursed as he headed back to his truck to drop off his hammer.

***

Maxine sat in the back of the strip club with a bottle of Hennessy on her table and a stripper with a super-fat ass on her lap. "So what you doing later?"

"Depends on what you trying to do later," the stripper said in a seductive tone. She licked her lips. She wasn't really into the girl-on-girl thing, but was willing to make an exception if the money was right.

"I'm trying to get you home with me," Maxine said, rubbing and squeezing on the stripper's ass.

The stripper ran her fingers through Maxine's hair. "As long as you willing to pay how you weigh, then we won't have a problem."

"Money ain't nothing, ma," Maxine said, flashing a big knot of money.

"What time you get off?"

"In about three more hours." The stripper made her ass clap in Maxine's face, getting her even more excited.

"A'ight, that's a bet." Maxine smiled as she sprinkled some singles on the stripper's ass before giving it a smack.

After Maine finished getting patted down for the second time, he was finally allowed to enter the club.

Maine smiled when he saw all the exotic half-naked women floating around the place. "Damn! Just what the fuck I needed." He walked over to a small table and helped himself to a seat.

When the waitress finally came over to him, he ordered a bottle of Hennessy and a Pepsi. After he placed his order, a dark-skinned stripper quickly invaded his space.

"What's a fine-ass man doing sitting over here all by himself?" she asked.

"Just scoping the place out." Maine was straining his neck to see how fat the stripper's ass was. "What's your name, ma?"

"Almond Joy," she answered, running her hands down his chest. "Can I give you a lap dance?" she whispered in Maine's ear, making sure she licked his earlobe before bringing her head back.

"Yeah, bring that big fat ass over here," Maine said, both of his hands on her hips.

The waitress returned with his bottle of Hennessy and Pepsi.

"Good looking, ma. Bring me back three hundred singles," Maine said, handing her three hundred-dollar bills.

"You sure you can handle all of this?" Almond Joy bent all the way over, shaking and bouncing her big fat ass all in Maine's face.

Maine poured himself a drink, and just as he was about to take a sip, he looked up and saw Maxine sipping over in the corner, looking like a man, all up in some stripper's ear like some headphones. *Get the fuck outta here!* He smiled, not believing his eyes. He immediately pulled out his cell phone and called Young Mike.

On the third ring, he picked up.

"No," Young Mike answered, "didn't change my mind. I don't feel like partying."

"Fuck all that, nigga! You and Harlem get down to the strip club we went to for your birthday!" Maine said with authority. "That bitch Maxine is down here by HERSELF!"

"A'ight, we on our way right now."

"Hurry the fuck up, and call me when y'all outside."

"I got you," Young Mike said, ending the call.

"Damn, daddy! You wanna talk on the phone, with all this pussy in your face," Almond Joy said, gyrating her hips.

"My bad. Had to take of some business real quick."
Maine put his cell phone back in his pocket. "Now show
me what you working with," he said, never taking his
eyes off Maxine.

"Gimme a second." Almond Joy held up one finger
as she walked over and tapped another dancer on
her shoulder. She returned and introduced her friend
Sparkle.

Before Maine could even say hi, Almond Joy and
Sparkle started kissing and feeling on one another.

Maine watched the two strippers make out right before his eyes. "That's what the fuck I'm talking about."

Sparkle, her legs spread wide open, sat on a chair
right next to Maine, while Almond Joy squatted down
and began eating her pussy like it was the last supper.

Maine sat back and enjoyed his front row seat. He
sprinkled singles all over Sparkle's and Almond Joy's
head as they performed.

Just as the show ended, Maine felt his phone vibrating. "Yooo," he answered.

"Yo, we outside," Young Mike said.

"A'ight. I'ma get the bitch to come outside, so be on
point." Maine hung up. "A yo, ma," he called out.

Sparkle came over toward Maine, a sexy smile on her
face. "What's up?"

"I gotta get up outta here, but I definitely need your
number before I go." Maine handed her his cell phone.

Sparkle took his phone and quickly punched in her
contact info inside the phone. "And you better call me
too!" she said, as she seductively turned and walked
over toward another john.

Maine took one more look at her ass jiggling as she
walked off. Then he locked her number in his phone
and downed the rest of his drink. "Yeah, I'ma tear that
pussy up," he said to himself as he stood up and headed
over to where Maxine was sitting.

Maxine was so busy rubbing all over the stripper, she didn't even see Maine approaching her. Maine walked right up to her, cocked back, and punched Maxine in the face, the impact from the blow causing Maxine's chair to tip over as she hit the floor.

"Think you can get away with robbing me, you filthy bitch!" Maine growled as he rained blow after blow on Maxine's exposed face. He then got up and started stomping her out, until a big bouncer came and tackled him to the ground.

"Get the fuck off me! I'ma kill this bitch!" Maine yelled as he struggled to break free from the bouncer's grip.

By now four big bouncers had him restrained, as people helped Maxine up to her feet.

"You a dead man," she said with a bloody smile. "You and your whole crew," she huffed, jerking her arms free. "Let me go. I'm fine."

Maxine exited the club. "Muthafuckas wanna play?" she said to herself as she power-walked to her car. She had an Uzi in her trunk and planned on letting off every single round, once she got her hands on it.

Just as she got close to her car, she heard multiple footsteps coming behind her. She quickly spun around, only to see two men wearing hoodies staring her down. She looked down and saw that both men were strapped.

"Aint this a bitch!" Maxine took a deep breath. She pulled out a cigarette, put it to her mouth, and lit it. A tear escaped from her eye. Right then and there, she knew she was about to die. "You know my boy Gruff gonna find y'all mufuckas, right?"

Young Mike sucked his teeth. "Fuck Gruff!" He raised his pistol and sent three hot slugs through her chest.

Once she hit the pavement, Harlem stood over her body and put two in her head. "Stupid-ass bitch!" he said, and him and Young Mike quickly fled the scene.

When Maine and the rest of the people in the club heard the gunshots, they all quickly ran out the club to see what just went down.

A smile quickly spread across Maine's face when he saw Maxine laid out in the middle of the street. "One down and one more to go," he said to himself, and he smoothly walked off to his car, feeling good with himself.

Chapter 15

"Damn! That shit was mad good." Detective Abraham rubbed his stomach, as him and Tom exited the soul food restaurant.

"Yeah, that was pretty good. I must say so myself," Tom replied, trying to be down. "So what we gonna do about this Ice Cube mufucka?"

"You mean Ice-T," Detective Abraham corrected him.

"Whatever the fuck his name is, you know who I'm talking about," Tom said in a drunken slur.

"Well, basically, we about to start running down on him and let him know that we still run shit," Detective Abraham said. "Harass him a li'l, bust his balls here and there, just to show him who's really in charge."

"You know I'm down." Tom slipped a cigarette between his lips. He didn't like black people, so to him it really didn't matter.

"Come on, let's go fuck with some of his peoples right now," Detective Abraham said as they headed for the car.

Just as Detective Abraham reached the passenger side door, he saw a van pull up alongside the car. Immediately, the back door slid open, and inside he saw a van full of niggas with red flags covering their faces.

Detective Abraham quickly ducked down as he heard about eight to nine different guns going off at the same time. "What the fuck!" he said in a panic, pulling out his .44.

Right after the gunfire ended, and Detective Abraham heard the tires on the van burning rubber as it pulled off. He stood to his feet and walked around the car and saw Tom laid out with about twenty holes in his body. He then turned and looked at the driver's side door, and it looked like Swiss cheese.

"These muthafuckas wanna play," he said, looking down at Tom's dead bullet-filled body. "I promise, I'ma make them pay for this."

Serena sat on the couch sipping on some wine, the cordless phone sitting right next to her. Every day Tone called her at the same time. Right on cue, the phone rang, and she picked it up on the second ring. "Hey, baby," she sang happily.

"What is my sexy-ass woman doing right now?" Tone asked.

Serena could see him smiling through the phone. "Sitting by the phone, waiting for my daddy to call me."

"Damn! I know you looking sexy, right," Tone said, licking his lips.

"I'ma take some pictures for you tonight and send them out to you tomorrow." Serena knew that the smallest thing meant so much in jail, so she planned on doing whatever she had to do to keep her man happy and focused.

"I can't wait. What you getting into today?"

"Well, right now I'm waiting for Maine to swing by and drop off some money. Then I'ma probably go get my hair done."

"Listen, I don't just want you sitting around the house. Why don't you go out and get some air tonight?"

"Nah, that's not really my flow. I like just chilling. I might go back home next week for a few days and go visit my father and the rest of my family."

"Sound good to me. Just keep me posted on your whereabouts. Don't just want you sitting around wasting your life 'cause I'm not around."

"You got it, daddy," Serena said as she heard the automatic recording say, *"You have one minute remaining."*

"Do what you gotta do, and I'ma holla back tomorrow."

"Okay, baby, be careful in there. I love you so much!"

"I love you too, baby. I'ma scream at you later," Tone said, ending the conversation.

As soon as Serena hung up the phone, she heard somebody knocking at her door. "Who is it?" she yelled, walking toward the front door. Serena looked through the peephole and saw Maine standing on the other side of the door.

"Hey, Maine," she said, stepping to the side so he could enter. "What's up?"

"What's good? How you been?"

"Everything been good. I can't complain."

"That's what's up." Maine handed her a book bag. "That's the re-up and y'all's profit in there."

"Thanks. I'll be sure to let Tone know everything is straight." Serena peeked inside the book bag.

"A'ight, if you need anything, holla at me." And Maine turned and headed for the door.

Once Maine left, Serena got dressed and headed out the door. She needed to get her hair, feet, and eyebrows done. Her first stop was the hair salon.

Serena stepped inside the salon, and the first person she saw was Mya. It just so happened that all the other beauticians were already busy with a client.

"You need your hair done?" Mya asked, standing behind her chair.

"Yes, I need my hair done, but I'm telling you right now—If you fuck my hair up, we going to have a serious problem!" Serena said, rolling her eyes.

"Girl, sit in this chair. Ain't nobody going to mess up your hair. I'm a professional."

"I hope so." Serena sat on the chair.

"So what can I do for you?"

"Just a wash and set."

"So how is Tone holding up in there?" Mya asked, as she began working on Serena's hair. Even though the two of them weren't still together, she still did care for him and often found herself worrying about him.

"He's fine. Just hanging in there."

For the rest of the time, the two women just chitchatted and got to know one another. By the time Serena's hair was finished, she had a new friend.

Ice-T stood on the porch of his hangout house just chilling with about fifteen soldiers all wearing something but red. "Damn! It's hot as fuck out here," he said, removing his shirt and exposing his cut-up abs and all the tattoos that covered his body. He fired up a blunt as he saw Nut and about six soldiers strolling to the porch.

"What's good? How things went out there?" Ice-T asked.

Nut told him, "We dropped one cop and sent a crazy loud message."

"What about Detective Abraham?" Ice-T asked.

"Bitch-ass nigga went running and hiding behind a car like a scared little bitch." Nut gave another soldier dap.

"I knew he was a bitch," Ice-T said, shaking his head. "He try to act up again, and I'ma need you to finish him off, straight up."

"I got you." Nut noticed mad police cars pulling up in front of the porch. "Everybody clean?" he asked.

"Yeah," Ice-T replied. "It's just two AK's over there on the side of the porch. One of the soldiers can hold that down, though." Ice-T watched Detective Abraham lead the pack toward the house.

Detective Abraham yelled, "Everybody down on the ground!"

Ice-T and his crew didn't budge.

"Get on the ground for what?" one of the soldiers asked.

Immediately, Detective Abraham broke his jaw with the butt of his .44. "I said, 'Everybody on the fuckin' ground!'" he yelled again, and him and his fellow officers began tossing people on the ground and handcuffing them.

When Detective Abraham reached Ice-T, he lifted him up to his feet so the two could be face to face. "That shit you pulled earlier was real cute." Detective Abraham smiled. "The only problem is, I'm untouchable." He head-butted Ice-T in his face then kneed him in his nuts.

Detective Abraham smiled as he watched Ice-T melt to the ground in pain. "I see I'ma have to teach you young punks some damn respect," he said, stomping on Ice-T's head like he was a roach.

Afterwards he grabbed Ice-T by his legs and dragged him off the porch and all the way to the squad car by his feet.

"Put this piece of shit in the car and hold him downtown until I fuckin' get there!" Detective Abraham ordered.

Gruff got off the bus and looked at his watch. He knew something was wrong because Maxine was never late, no matter what. He pulled out his cell phone and dialed her number. Straight to voice mail. He tried again, only to get the same result.

"Fuck!" he cursed loudly as he quickly flagged down a cab.

He paid the cab driver and got out in front of the run-down motel where she last said she would be staying while he was gone. He pulled out one of his 9s and kicked open the room door. He stepped inside and turned on the lights. He scanned the entire room before putting away his 9. Gruff looked around and saw Maxine's .357 sitting on the dresser. Immediately he knew she was dead, 'cause she never left her favorite gun just sitting around, unless she was only gonna be gone for a little while.

"Muthafuckas!" Gruff said loudly. He didn't know who did what, but he definitely was about to find out.

Gruff pulled up in front of the corner store, where about eight guys stood. They looked like they was selling something. Gruff took one last pull of his cigarette, flicked it out the window, cocked back one of his 9s, and slid out the car. He walked up on the curb and fired two shots. His two targets dropped to the ground holding their leg, and the rest of the men ran for their lives.

Gruff walked right up to the first man and placed the barrel to his forehead. "Who killed Maxine?" he growled.

"Huh?"

The last thing the man heard was the sound of Gruff's 9 blasting. He immediately moved on to the next man. "Who killed Maxine?"

"I don't know no Maxine. Please don't kill—"

Gruff pulled the trigger—*Boom!*—and walked back to his car and drove off like nothing ever happened. He didn't know who had killed his partner, but he was damn sure going to find out.

***

Two days later Ice-T and his crew were finally released.

"Hey, daddy," one of his girls said as he slid in the
passenger seat of the truck.

"Take me home," Ice-T said in an angry tone.

The chick wanted to ask him was he all right, but she
decided to just keep her mouth shut and do as she was
told.

As soon as Ice-T walked in his house, he walked
straight over to the phone and placed a hit on Detective
Abraham. "Muthafucka think he can just do shit any
ol' kinda way. He got another thing coming," he said
out loud. Detective Abraham had just messed with the
wrong one.

"Tell my man what you just told me," Harlem said,
putting the fiend on the spot in front of Young Mike.

"I heard through the grapevine that Gruff out here
looking for the person who killed his lady friend," Malcolm reported.

"Who the fuck told you that shit?" Young Mike asked,
not believing the drug addict standing in front of him.

"I was in the store trying to steal some potato chips
when I heard a few shots go off," Malcolm said. "I ran
to the door and peeked out and saw him ask one of the
guys who killed his friend, and when the man told him
he didn't know, he blew his head off right there in front
of the store."

"Nigga, you sure?" Young Mike asked again. He
knew fiends would say just about anything for a hit.

"Positive, my brother," Malcolm replied. "Now is
y'all gon' hook me up or what?"

Young Mike reached down in his pocket and handed
the fiend a ten-dollar bill. "Now get the fuck outta
here!" He gave Malcolm a shove 'cause he wasn't walking fast enough.

"You believe that nigga?" Harlem asked.

"Shit! I don't know what to believe," Young Mike said. "Just be on point, just in case."

"You know I stay strapped," Harlem said, reminding his friend how he got down. "That fiend was probably lying anyway."

"He probably was, but what if he wasn't?"

"Whatever. I'm about to go get high. You rollin'?" Harlem asked.

"Nah, I gotta go take care of a little something," Young Mike said, giving Harlem dap, and the two men went their separate ways.

"I don't care how you do it, as long as it gets done," Detective Abraham barked in the receiver of his cell phone. "The muthafucka tried to have me killed. Now it's his turn to get put in the ground!"

Detective Abraham stepped out the station and walked around the corner to where his car was parked and saw it burnt up. "What the fuck? This muthafucka is good." He smiled as he examined his burnt up car. He quickly picked up his cell phone and dialed Maine's number.

"What up?" Maine answered.

"Meet me downtown at our other spot in an hour," Detective Abraham said before hanging up.

About forty-five minutes later Maine pulled up across the street from the new stash crib. When he reached the door, he did the special code knock, and a worker opened the door and let him in.

"What's good, Li'l Man?" Maine said, giving the younger man dap. "How them weekly numbers been looking?"

"They been looking wonderful," Detective Abraham answered from over on the couch, where he was sitting. "Ever since we been getting this new product from Serena, our numbers been shooting through the roof."

"Speaking of numbers, I gotta go hit shorty in a few days," Maine said, reminding himself out loud.

"Who? Serena?" Detective Abraham asked, his face crumpled up.

"Yeah, she is the only lead to the connect," Maine reminded him.

"Fuck that bitch! We gon' short change her on this go-around." Detective Abraham fanned the air. "We doing all the work any mu'fuckin' way."

Maine asked, "But then, what if she stop getting the work for us 'cause that paper ain't right?"

"She ain't gon' trip 'cause she so in love with Tone. She won't dare do nothing to piss him off, so basically we got this bitch in the palm of our hands," Detective Abraham said, a wicked smile on his face.

"Damn! But what if Tone get mad 'cause he's getting shorted?"

"Let me worry about all that. As long as you getting your money, what does it matter?"

"That's some fucked-up shit," Maine said. "But you right—This a wolf business."

"Exactly. But I called you down here for something else."

"What's up?"

"This Ice-T muthafucka is out of control, and he need to be dealt with as soon as possible."

"I don't know," Maine said, scratching his head. "That might be kind of hard. Every time he step out the house, he be at least twenty deep."

"I know." Detective Abraham paused. "We going to have to find away to get at this clown, 'cause this muthafucka has to go."

"Give me about a week, and I'll figure something out." Maine looked at his watch.

"If you don't come up with nothing, then I'ma have to take matters into my own hands," Detective Abraham said. "And when I do that, the shit going to get real messy."

Maine got up to leave. "Give me a week, and I'll have something for you."

"Damn! Where you rushing off to?" Detective Abraham asked, noticing Maine kept on looking at his watch.

"Got a super-hot date tonight with this chick I met." Maine smiled. "All this business, I haven't even had a chance to get no pleasure." He winked.

"Handle your business." Detective Abraham gave Maine a pound, followed by a hug. "Just make sure you wrap it up."

"Always," Maine replied, as he exited the stash crib.

After making sure everything was running smoothly and all the money was right, Detective Abraham exited the stash crib. "Damn! I'm tired as fuck!" He yawned as he pulled off.

For the entire ride home, all Detective Abraham could think about was doing harm to Ice-T. He was so caught up in his thoughts, he almost ran a red light.

Detective Abraham cursed when he saw a bum walking up to his ride with some kind of liquid in a bottle and a dirty-looking newspaper in his hand. "Awww shit!" He hated when bums came up to his car trying to wash his windows. The bum sprayed the liquid on the windshield and began wiping away.

"Yo, I don't need that!" Detective Abraham yelled. "Get the fuck away from my car!" He beeped the horn so the bum could move. But the bum continued to wash the front windshield like that was his nine-to-five.

Detective Abraham pulled out his .44 and hopped out the car. "Muthafucka, didn't I tell you to get away from my car?" He slammed the bum on top of his hood and placed the gun to his head. He thought about pulling the trigger, until he realized the bum was his son.

"Malcolm?" he said, releasing the strong hold he had on him.

Malcolm struggled to get free. "Get the fuck off me!"

"I should've put a fuckin' bullet in your head and put you out your fuckin' misery." Detective Abraham shook his head in disgust at Malcolm. "All this money out here, and you wanna be out here getting high and shit."

"You got some nerve," Malcolm said through clenched teeth. "You the one that got me hooked on this shit in the first place. I should be the one putting a bullet in your head!"

"Testing your product and being a fiend is two different things." Detective Abraham smirked. "You just a weak muthafucka, point-blank."

"Don't you even worry about me," Malcolm said with a smile. "My god told me everything is going to be all right, and my god is a forgiving god."

Detective Abraham smiled as he dug down into his pocket and pulled out two twenty bags of coke he had taken from the stash house. "Nigga, this is your god right here," he said, holding up the two bags. "Here, take this. I know you want it, you fuckin' junkie!"

Malcolm walked up to his father, took the drugs from his hands, turned and walked off into the night singing an old-school gospel song.

"Stupid-ass junkie." Detective Abraham hopped back in his car and headed home.

Gruff looked over at Tiger. "Let's go handle this business."

The two hopped out the car and swiftly walked over to the building he was looking for. Gruff walked in the building and through the lobby toward the staircase.

Tenants in the lobby waiting for the elevator quickly jumped back when they saw the big pit bull roaming free without a leash.

Gruff hit the steps, skipping two at a time, until he reached the fifth floor. He then pulled out his twin 9 mm's and walked to the apartment he was looking for. He aimed his 9 at the lock and pulled the trigger then came forward with a kick, forcing the door open.

When the fat man sitting on the couch saw Gruff kick open his front door, his eyes got as big as saucers. He quickly turned to grab the pistol he always left under the cushion of the couch, but Gruff aimed his 9 and pulled the trigger.

The fat man immediately clutched his bloody arm and rolled onto the floor. "What the fuck, man!" he yelled. "What the fuck you want from me?"

"I know you keep your ear to the street." Gruff slipped a cigarette between his lips. "Who killed my road dog?"

"Who the fuck is your road dog?" the fat man asked, a confused look on his face.

"Stop playing stupid, muthafucka!" Gruff said, his cigarette dangling with each word he spoke. "Maxine, who killed her?"

"I don't know."

Gruff let a bullet rip through his thigh.

"Awwwwww shit!" he howled in pain.

"Last time I'ma ask you," Gruff said, a plain look on his face. He was sick and tired of playing games with the fat man.

"Man, I swear to God, I don't know who did that shit, but I swear if you let me live, I'll definitely find out for you."

Gruff smirked. "You gon' find out for me?"

"I swear to God," the fat man said in a begging tone.

Gruff sicced his dog on the fat man. "Get him, Tiger!"
And he sat back and watched as Tiger ripped the fat
man apart like it was nothing.

Once the fat man was dead, Gruff yelled, "That's
enough!" and Tiger immediately stopped what she was
doing and returned back to his master's side. "Come
on, girl, let's go," Gruff said, and him and Tiger exited
the apartment.

Maine and Sparkle was chilling in his living room,
sipping on some wine. This was the first time he had
Sparkle alone, and couldn't wait to break her off.

"For a minute I was thinking you wasn't going to call
me," Sparkle said, rolling her eyes at him.

He licked his lips. "My bad. I just been like super
busy. Know what I mean?"

"Mmm-hmm." Sparkle sucked her teeth. "Tell me
anything."

"Don't act like that. As sexy as you was looking at the
club that night, you know you was going to get a phone
call from me."

Sparkle crossed her legs, exposing her pretty feet.
"Well, it took you long enough."

"All that matters is that you here now," Maine said,
undressing Sparkle with his eyes.

"Your crib is nice. I sure wish I could get around this
joint."

"You got it," Maine said as he refilled both of their
glasses with wine. He stood up and began giving her a
tour of his crib.

After showing Sparkle the whole house, he finally
showed her the master bedroom. "Here's where I
sleep," he said, patting the bed.

"That bed looks mad comfortable. Maybe one day
you might let me sleep on it." She seductively sipped
on her wine.

Maine whipped out his dick. "Fuck the bullshit!"

"Damn!" Sparkle sat her wineglass on the dresser and immediately slid down to her knees. "It's about time." She made sure she spread his legs wide apart, so she could really go to work on him.

Sparkle started out licking all over Maine's dick before she took the whole thing in her mouth. She made loud slurping noises as she sucked the shit outta his dick, using one hand to jerk his dick and the other to juggle his balls.

Sparkle felt Maine's dick swell up, and immediately she stopped. "No, I don't want you to come yet, not until you feel this wet pussy." She stood up and began wiggling out of her jeans.

Maine just sat back on the bed and sipped on his wine as Sparkle stripped for him. Just from the way she moved on the dance floor the other night at the club, he already knew she had some good pussy.

"Daddy, I'ma need you to taste this good pussy!" Sparkle lay back on the bed, her legs spread wide open.

A perverted smile spread across Maine's face as he quickly stripped down butt naked. He walked over to her and poured a little bit of his wine on her freshly waxed pussy and quickly sucked it off. Then he poured some more on it and repeated the process, licking and sucking all over Sparkle's pussy like he owned it.

Once Maine was sure she had come twice, he decided to introduce her to the back shots. He rolled on a condom and smoothly slid inside of her. Sparkle took both of her hands and spread both of her ass cheeks open, giving Maine better access to the pussy. Maine grabbed a handful of Sparkle's hair, pulling her head back as he thrust himself in and out of her fat, wet pussy, until he exploded in the condom.

"Damn, daddy! I ain't know it was like that," Sparkle said, laid across the bed butt naked and her eyes closed.

"Damn! That was some good-ass pussy," Maine said as he drifted off.

Gruff sat in a car across the street from where Maxine was murdered. He turned up his bottle of Hennessy as he waited patiently for the person he was looking for to exit the club.

An hour and a half later a big bouncer exited the club and flagged down a cab. Gruff quickly made the engine come to life with a turn of the key and followed the cab all the way to Brooklyn.

The bouncer slid out the cab and fumbled around in his pocket for his keys.

"Just the man I been looking for," Gruff said, holding his 9 mm down to his side.

The bouncer looked at the gun Gruff held in his hand, then down at the big vicious-looking pit bull. "What's this all about?" he said nervously, throwing up his hands in surrender.

"I'll ask all the questions." Gruff moved in closer. "Open the mu'fuckin' door!" He pushed the big man through the lobby door. "What floor you live on?"

"The third."

When they reached the bouncer's apartment, Gruff put a bullet in his leg and watched the big man drop like a tree.

"Please don't kill me," the bouncer pleaded. "Please, I have a family," he said, crying like a bitch.

"I'm going to ask you a simple question. You give me the answer I'm looking for, and you get to live. You give me the answer I'm not looking for, and you see my friend here"—he nodded over at Tiger—"you going to be her dinner. So it's all on you, whether you live or die."

The bouncer looked over at Tiger. "I'll tell you whatever you want to know. Just please don't kill me."

"Who killed my partner Maxine?" Gruff lit up a cigarette.

"Who's Maxine?"

"The girl that was killed outside of your club, nigga," Gruff growled. "Don't play stupid!"

"Oooh, her," the bouncer said, thinking back. "She got into a fight with this guy inside the club."

"What guy?" Gruff asked quickly.

"I can't remember his name, but I remember the guy walked right up to her and snuffed her out of her chair."

"I need a name." Gruff flicked his cigarette on the floor. "Think hard."

The bouncer was sweating bullets. "I'm trying to think."

"You got ten seconds."

The bouncer suddenly remembered. "Maine. That's his name—Maine."

A smile spread across Gruff's face. "Maine did this?"

"Yeah, it was him."

"You sure?"

"Positive," the bouncer said, wiping the sweat from his forehead.

"And you said you sure, right?" Gruff asked again.

"Positive. I swear to God, it was Maine who did that shit."

"A'ight, good looking. I appreciate the info. Sorry about your leg," Gruff said as he turned and made his exit.

Chapter 16

"Yeah, I heard it's going down out there in them streets," Styles said as him and Tone stepped outside and walked the yard. Styles was Tone's cell mate. Before he went in, he was doing some decent numbers on the streets, but due to a snitch, he found himself behind the wall.

"Damn! Shit popping off out there like that?" Tone asked.

"Yeah, I heard that nigga Ice-T tried to get your pops murdered, but niggas said your pops did some matrix shit and somehow got away," Styles said, repeating what he was told.

"Word?"

"Yeah. Then I heard Maine bodied that Maxine chick in broad daylight."

"Get the fuck outta here!" Tone said in disbelief. Since he had been locked up, nobody from the outside was keeping him up-to-date on what was going on out in the streets.

"Word. When the last time you spoke to them niggas?"

"It's been a minute," Tone admitted, but he didn't stress it 'cause he knew his team was out taking care of business. And, besides, he would be going home shortly.

"You gon' have to get your ears back to the streets," Styles told him. "Shit not no game out here. 'Cause when I go home, I'm climbing that ladder back to the top. I can't fuck with that being broke shit."

"You ain't the only one." Tone noticed a fight break out in the middle of the yard. He shook his head as he watched two inmates fight over a basketball game. "Dumb broke-ass niggas! I gotta hurry up and get the fuck up outta here."

"Shit! You'll be outta here in no time. You only got eighteen months left." Styles jumped up and grabbed the pull-up bar and began doing a set.

"Fuck that! I wanna go home now." Tone was tired looking around and only seeing niggas.

"The key is, when you get out, to make sure you stay out." Styles hopped off the bar.

"Yeah, you right," Tone said, in deep thought.

Styles snapped his fingers to get Tone's attention. "Fuck you over there thinking about?"

"Thinking about Serena and a whole lot of other shit."

"What's on your mind?"

"Mya had my son, and I still haven't seen him yet." Tone exhaled.

"Have you wrote her or tried to get in contact with her?"

"I tried to call once," Tone said, "but her punk-ass boyfriend didn't accept the call."

"So she probably don't even know you tried to get in contact with her."

"Fuck it!" Tone huffed. "I'm heading back in, so I can call my baby." He walked off and headed inside.

Once inside Tone picked up the phone and dialed Serena's number. On the third ring, she picked up.

"Hey, babyyyyy," she sang.

"Hey, baby. Where the fuck you at?" Tone was hearing mad noise in the background.

"I'm out here in Los Angeles. I had the house phone calls forwarded to my cell phone."

"Oh. A'ight. What? You got a little homesick?"

"Nah. My father called me the other day and said he needed to talk to me about something, so we about to find out what's up."

"You think he found out what you and your uncle been doing?"

"Nah," Serena answered quickly. "I know my father, and if it was that, trust me, we would both know." She chuckled.

"A'ight, cool. You just make sure you be careful out there."

"You know I am, baby, and as soon as I get back, I'm coming to see you." Serena smiled.

"Good. 'Cause right about now I need to see you," Tone told her. "I'm going to give you the biggest hug ever."

"Awww, baby! You in there missing me? That's so cute."

"I can't wait to get up outta here. This shit is the worst."

"You don't got much longer to go," Serena said as she pulled up in front of her father's mansion. "Will you be able to call me later?"

"Definitely. Go handle your business," Tone said. "Oh, hold up. I need you to do me a favor."

"Anything."

Serena slid out the rental car and walked up to the front of her father's house.

"If you can, can you try to get Mya to bring the baby up here to see me?"

"I got you, baby. As soon as I get back to New York, I'll get on it."

"Thanks, baby. I love the shit outta you."

"I love you too, daddy. Call me later." Serena blew a kiss through the phone.

"I got you, baby."

"Talk to you later." Serena hung up her cell phone and rang the doorbell, and a short Spanish man answered the door, holding an AK.

"Hey, Jose." Serena leaned in for a hug.

"Serena, what you doing here?" Jose said, shocked to see Serena standing in front of him.

"My father asked me to come out here and see him. So how you been?"

"You know," Jose said, nodding toward his AK, "still making sure your father is safe."

"Damn!" Serena said to herself. For as long as she could remember, Jose had been her father's personal bodyguard slash hit man.

"Your father is in his office. You remember where it's at, right?"

"Yeah, I remember where it's at." Serena walked down the hallway toward the office and knocked lightly on the door.

"Come in!" Santiago yelled from behind his desk. The biggest smile appeared on his face when he saw his only child step into his office.

"Hey, Daddy," Serena sang as she slid in her father's arms.

"Shit! I thought you got lost for a second," Santiago joked. "How was your flight?"

"It was cool." Serena sat down on the sofa that rested up against the wall. "So what's so important that I had to fly down here on such short notice?"

Santiago sat down behind his desk before he replied. "I need to talk to you about this new boyfriend you got."

"What about him?" Serena asked.

"I heard he was black," Santiago said, staring a hole through his daughter with his eyes.

"Yes, he is black, and?"

"What you mean, *and*?" Santiago frowned. "You know I don't approve of you being with a *moreno*."

Serena sucked her teeth. "Well, that's why I didn't ask for your approval."

"I taught you better than that." Santiago shook his head. "Them blacks can't be trusted, and you know it."

"You never even gave 'em a chance."

"Give 'em a chance to do what? Snitch on me?" Santiago laughed. "Never you trust them if you want to"

"Well, I do trust him, and he's a nice guy. I can't wait for you to meet him."

"I don't think you understand." Santiago stood up.

"No. You don't understand that I'm grown now. And if I want to be with somebody, whether he's black or not, that's my business!" she yelled.

"You know what? You right. You're grown, and I can't tell you what to do." He paused. "But let me tell you what I can do." A smile spread across his face. "I can make you a promise."

"What promise?" Serena asked curiously.

"I promise you that if anything ever happens to you 'cause of those animals you around, I promise I will kill every last one of them!"

"Why can't you just be happy for me? You always gotta try to find something negative about everything."

"I am happy for you," Santiago said, forcing a smile. "I'm just letting you know how I feel," he said with a raised eyebrow.

"Whatever!" Serena shot to her feet and stormed out of her father's house, headed back to the airport.

"Here you go," Serena said, handing the cab driver a fifty-dollar bill. "Keep the change," she said as she slid out the back of the cab.

As she walked up to her front door, she saw Malcolm standing on the steps in front of the door. "Hey, Malcolm. How's it going?"

"I been okay," Malcolm said, flashing his rotten-tooth smile. "I was looking for my brother. Do you know when he'll be back in?"

"Your brother is in jail," Serena told him. "He been in there for almost two years now."

"For real?" Malcolm said, scratching his head.

"Yeah, it's been that long," Serena said as she unlocked her front door. "You want something to eat or something?"

"If you don't mind."

"A'ight. Have a seat, and I'll be back in a second. I gotta pee," Serena said, jogging to the downstairs bathroom.

She returned to the living room a few minutes later, but she didn't see Malcolm. "Malcolm!" she called out. "Where you at?"

"I'm right here!" Malcolm said from behind her as he busted Serena over the head with a glass vase.

Serena hit the floor and immediately felt her warm blood running down the back of her neck.

"Where's the money at?" Malcolm barked. He kicked Serena in the face with his dirty-ass sneakers. He snatched Serena back up to her feet by her hair, and he swung with all his might and punched her in the face.

"Where's the money at, bitch?"

Serena quickly kneed Malcolm in his nuts and ran to the kitchen, where she grabbed a butcher's knife from off the rack. "Come on, muthafucka!" she said through a pair of busted lips, holding out the knife and inching toward the crackhead.

Once she got close enough, she jabbed Malcolm in the stomach with the knife, but before she could bring her arm back, Malcolm grabbed her wrist and quickly disarmed her. Then he flung his head forward full force and head-butted Serena in her face then hip-tossed her through the kitchen table.

Malcolm looked over and saw Serena's purse lying on the floor. He snatched it up and ran out the front door.

"Oh my God!" Serena cried as she lay on top of the broken glass.

"Fuck is we going to Tone crib for if he in jail?" Harlem asked from the passenger seat.

"'Cause he asked me to check up on his girl every now and then." Young Mike pulled into Tone's driveway and saw the front door wide open. Immediately he knew something was wrong.

"Why the fuck is the door wide open like that?" Harlem asked.

"We 'bout to find out," Young Mike said as he slid out the whip, his .357 already drawn. He walked up to the front door with caution. "Anybody in here?" Young Mike yelled, inching his way inside the house, Harlem close on his heels.

Young Mike didn't see anything, but he heard what sounded like a woman crying.

When he turned the corner, he saw Serena lying in a pile of glass crying. "Oh shit!" Young Mike ran and knelt down by Serena's side.

"I'ma check the rest of the crib and make sure ain't nobody still up in here." Harlem began searching the crib for a would-be attacker.

Young Mike quickly called an ambulance. "They on they way," he said as he helped her out of all the broken glass. "Who did this shit to you?"

"Malcolm," Serena said, wincing in pain.

"Who the fuck is Malcolm?"

Serena didn't even answer. She was in too much pain to hold a conversation.

"Ain't nobody in here but us." Harlem stuck his gun back in his waistband.

Fifteen minutes later the ambulance arrived and escorted Serena to the hospital.

Gruff pointed at the beautiful woman. "Is that the bitch right there?"

"Yeah, that's her," the bouncer confirmed.

"A'ight. I'll be right back." Gruff slid out the driver's seat, Tiger right on his heels. "Excuse me, miss," Gruff called out.

Sparkle looked back and saw a man with a big-ass dog trying to get her attention. When she realized she didn't know the man, she kept on walking. *Where's my Mace?* She fumbled around in her purse looking for the pepper spray.

Seconds later Sparkle felt a hand grab her shoulder.

Gruff shoved his 9 mm into Sparkle's back. "Bitch, scream and I'll blow your fuckin' titty off!"

"What do you want from me?" Sparkle asked.

"Shut the fuck up!" Gruff roughly escorted Sparkle back to his car. He opened up the trunk, forced her inside then slammed the trunk shut. Then he got back in the driver's seat and pulled off.

Styles hopped up from off the floor after doing some push-ups. "What's good? You coming to the yard today?"

"Nah, not right now. The police just told me I had a visit," Tone replied, throwing on his Polo shirt that he only wore on visits.

"A'ight, my nigga. Do your thing." Styles gave Tone a pound. "I'ma head to the yard and go get in a quick workout."

"A'ight. I'ma scream at you when I get back."

Tone exited his cell and walked over to the C.O.'s desk, so he could be escorted down to the visiting room. He stepped in the visiting room and quickly spotted Serena.

"Why the fuck she got on those dark-ass shades?" Tone asked himself, but as he got closer and closer, he could see the swelling all over her face. "What the fuck happened to your face?" he growled as soon as he sat down.

"Your brother attacked me," Serena said, breaking down in tears.

"What happen?"

"I got back from seeing my father, and I saw Malcolm standing outside our door," Serena began. "So I let him in and offered him some food. Next thing you know, he attacked me from behind and took my purse."

"Why the fuck is you letting that muthafucka in the house when I'm not home?"

"Because he's your brother, that's why. What was I supposed to do?"

"I'm gonna kill that nigga as soon as I get up outta here." Tone banged on the table with his fist.

Serena was about to say something until she saw a big C.O. walk over. "Is everything all right over here?" he asked, looking at Serena.

"Yes, we're fine," she replied.

"Yeah, we fine," Tone said, and the big C.O. walked off.

"From now on, I don't want nobody in that fuckin' house except Maine, and that's only when he's dropping off money."

"Okay, daddy," Serena said. "Are you mad at me?"

"No, I'm not mad at you."

"Sorry for letting him in the house. I just thought that, 'cause he was your brother, it was okay."

"Brother or not, he's still a fuckin' crackhead," Tone reminded her. "And you know they'll do whatever they have to do to get that fix. Don't put nothing past nobody. Always protect yourself."

"Next time, I promise I will."

"Don't let it be no next time," Tone said, mad that his woman's face was all bruised up. "I'm still going to kill that muthafucka when I get up out of here."

"He's not even worth it," Serena said, trying to talk Tone out of it.

"You just stay the fuck out of harm's way until I get up outta here, 'cause if something happens to you, I'ma have to go on a killing spree."

"I got you, baby. I promise I won't put myself in harm's way again."

Just then, the same big C.O. walked up and announced that the visit was over.

"I'm going to call you tonight around eight o'clock." Tone hugged Serena tight and tongued her down.

"I love so much, baby. Call me!" Serena yelled over her shoulder as she exited the visiting room.

Tone made it back to his housing unit and spotted Styles.

"Everything straight with the old lady?" Styles asked, giving Tone a pound.

"Nah. My fuckin' junkie-ass brother damn near beat her half to death for her pocketbook." Tone helped himself to a seat.

"Get the fuck outta here! Nigga, you serious?"

"Dead serious," Tone huffed. "You know I'm going to kill that nigga when I get out, right?"

"Shit, I'll help you." Styles laughed.

Tone was getting ready to say something, until some big, strong, box-head-looking guy walked up and interrupted their conversation.

"Yo, fam, you in my seat!"

Box Head was a little too aggressive for Tone's liking. Tone looked up at the big man. "Ay, yo, fam, the seat was empty when I sat down."

"Bullshit! I left my fuckin' ID on top of the seat!" Box Head said.

Tone got up a little and looked under his ass. No ID was there. "Fam, ain't no ID on this seat."

"Yeah, nigga, that's 'cause you moved my shit!" Box Head pulled up his pants like he was ready to get busy.

"It's another chair right there," Tone said, nodding toward the empty chair right next to him.

"I don't want that chair. I want my chair, muthafucka!"

Tone jumped up with quickness and caught Box Head with a two-piece. The two punches had no effect on Box Head, who grabbed Tone in a bear hug and belly-to-belly slammed him down the floor.

All the inmates erupted in a loud "Ooooh!" when they saw Tone's body get slammed to the floor.

Just as Box Head was about to pound Tone out, Styles came with the thick dictionary and smacked Box Head across the face with it. Once Tone made it back to his feet, it was on. Him and Box Head got it on like they was fighting in the UFC, going blow for blow, until Styles jumped in, turning it to a two-on-one. But Box Head still held his own, taking more punches than he delivered, but yet he stayed on his feet, which was amazing, for the kind of blows he was taking.

Within seconds, ten "turtles" came rushing in and beat the three men down with nightsticks until each man was laid out. Then they escorted them to the box.

***

"Wake up, bitch!" Gruff yelled, slashing a glass of water in Sparkle's face.

Sparkle opened her eyes and found herself lying on a dirty ground in some kind of warehouse. "Where am I?" she asked in a groggy voice.

CLICK-CLACK!

"I'm only going to ask you this once!" Gruff cocked his shotgun and sat it directly in her face. "Where can I find that nigga Maine at?"

"I don't know," Sparkle answered, still not fully understanding what was going on.

"That bitch is lying," the bouncer yelled. "I saw y'all exchange numbers."

"You a straight-up bitch!" Sparkle spat at the bouncer.

Gruff dug down in Sparkle's purse and removed her cell phone. He tossed the cell phone on her chest. "Call him right now!"

When Sparkle hesitated, Gruff pressed the barrel of the shotgun to her forehead. "Don't play with me!"

One peek at the shotgun, and Sparkle began dialing Maine's number.

Maine pulled up in front of Tone's crib. He grabbed the bottle of Grey Goose from off the floor and turned the bottle all the way up. Then he grabbed the book bag full of cash from off the front seat and headed toward the door.

"Hey, Maine. What's up?" Serena stepped to the side so he could enter.

"Just came by to drop off this bread." Maine stared at Serena, a hungry look in his eyes. "What happened to your face?"

Serena noticed the way Maine was looking at her. "I fell down the stairs."

"You need a man here to protect you." Maine sat down on the couch. "It's a lot of crazy people out here, and ain't no telling what they're capable of," he said with a raised eyebrow.

"Tone will be home shortly," Serena said, thumbing through the cash. "Hold up, this ain't right." She looked inside the book bag. "This shit is short."

"We took a few losses this month." Maine shrugged his shoulders.

Serena smirked, knowing they was only trying to jerk her because Tone wasn't there. "Yeah, a'ight. We'll see what Tone has to say about this."

Maine stood up to leave. "We'll make it up on the next go-around."

"Y'all come short one more time, and that's the end of y'all getting more of this good shit."

"Whatever," Maine said as he exited the crib.

He got back in his car and grabbed his Grey Goose bottle. He heard his cell phone ringing while he was taking a swig from the bottle. He looked at the phone and saw Sparkle's name flashing across the screen. "Sexy, what up?" he answered, pulling out of the driveway.

"Hey, daddy. What you doing right now right?" Sparkle asked, Gruff's shotgun pressed up against her forehead.

"About to go pick up some money. Why? What's up? You trying to see the god?"

"You know I am, daddy."

"A'ight. I might go out to the club tonight. Why don't you meet me there, so we can have a few drinks and chill."

"Nah, I don't really feel like partying tonight. I just need to hop on that dick and ride it real slow—backwards."

Just hearing those words got Maine's dick hard. "A'ight, so when you wanna do this?"

"I guess you can come pick me up in about a hour."

"At the same spot?"

"You know it." Sparkled laughed, trying to hide her nervousness.

"Say no more. I'll see you in a hour," Maine said, ending the call.

Gruff removed the barrel of his shotgun from Sparkle's forehead. "You did good."

"So what now?" she asked nervously.

"Nothing. I'm going to take you home, and that's it."

"Are you going to kill Maine?" she asked, fear in her eyes.

"Bitch!" Gruff barked as he turned and smacked the shit out of Sparkle. "You just better be thankful I don't shoot ya dumb ass!" He huffed, "Don't be asking me no muthafuckin' questions!"

"I'm sorry," Sparkle said, holding the side of her face.

"As a matter of fact come over here and suck my dick"—Gruff pulled out his dick—"since you got so much mouth."

Sparkle quickly swallowed her pride as she crawled over to Gruff and slipped his penis in her mouth and began sucking on it.

Maine pulled up a block away from Sparkle's crib so he could count his money before he picked her up. He rested his .380 on the passenger's seat as he began to get his count on. Once he was done, he pulled his cell phone and dialed Sparkle's number.

"Hello," she answered.

"Yo, come outside. I'm in the front." Maine hung up the phone as he put his car in drive and pulled up in front of Sparkle's crib.

"Come, bitch, don't take all muthafuckin' day," Maine huffed. When he looked up at his rearview mirror, he saw a figure wearing a hoodie creeping up on his car from behind at a fast speed. Immediately he threw the gear in drive and stomped on the gas.

When Gruff saw Maine's car start to move, he immediately raised his 9 mm sub-machine gun and opened fire.

Maine didn't get too far before he felt a bullet pierce the top of his shoulder. Seconds later, two more hot slugs ripped through the driver's seat and entered his back. "Awwww shit!" Maine screamed as he lost control of his vehicle and crashed into a light pole.

Seeing that, Gruff quickly reloaded his weapon and moved in for the kill.

Sparkle looked out her window and saw Gruff run up on Maine's car and open fire. "Oh my God!" she screamed. She ran upstairs and grabbed her .380 from her top drawer and quickly ran back downstairs.

As she ran down the steps, she heard a loud crash. "I'm coming, baby," she said to herself as she cleared the last step and flew out the front door. She reached her porch and saw Gruff creeping up on Maine's car from behind. She quickly aimed her gun in Gruff's direction and let off. *Pow! Pow! Pow! Pow!*

Gruff heard the shots and immediately got low and took cover behind a parked car. Once the shooting stopped, he sprang up from behind the parked car and aired Sparkle out. He watched as his bullets made the woman look like she was doing some kind of break dance before her body hit the ground. "Dumb-ass bitch!"

Gruff heard cop sirens getting louder and louder. He quickly emptied the rest of his clip in Maine's car as he backpedaled back to his car. Then he hopped in and burned rubber.

Tone walked out to the visiting room, and a big smile appeared across his face when he spotted his baby. "Hey, baby," Tone said, giving Serena a big kiss. "How you feeling?"

"Not too good," Serena said as she sat down.

"Talk to me. What's up?"

"Maine came to see me the other day and he was short with the money again."

"How short?"

"About ten thousand," Serena answered. "They only doing that because you in here."

"A'ight, this how we going to do this. They come up short again, and they don't get no more product."

Serena took a sip from her soda. "Then what are we going to do for money?"

"I'll think of something. I been trying to get in contact with my father, and he hasn't been taking my calls."

"What's that all about?"

"I don't know, but trust me, I'm going to find out," Tone said, holding on to Serena's hands. "Six more months and all this shit is over."

"I know. I been counting down every day."

"Don't you worry about nothing. I'ma take care of everything when I get home."

"I know you are, baby," Serena said, tears rolling down her face.

"Why you crying for, baby?"

"Because I miss you." Serena sobbed. "I been so lonely without you, it feels like my life is over. When you come home my life can finally start again."

"It's going to be okay. We done made it this far. This last six months ain't shit, but I need you to continue to stay strong for your king. Can you do that for me?"

Serena nodded her head yes. "I just want to jump across this table and fuck the shit out of you!" she said through clenched teeth.

"Don't talk to me like that." Tone bit his bottom lip. "You know that shit turns me the fuck on."

"It is so on when you get home."

Just then the C.O. announced the end of visiting hours.

"Six more months, baby." Tone hugged Serena tight, gripping both of her ass cheeks.

"I can't wait." Serena gave Tone a big juicy kiss before exiting the visiting room.

"You wanted to see us," Young Mike said, as him and Harlem stood side by side in front of Detective Abraham's desk.

"My boy Maine is laid up in the hospital right now, and I don't know how or why," Detective Abraham said. "They found a gun in his car, so he's under investigation and handcuffed to his fuckin' hospital bed. What I need y'all to do is go and get me some answers."

"I got you," Young Mike said.

"I don't care what y'all have to do to find some answers. Just do it!"

"I'm on it," Young Mike said, and him and Harlem hit the streets looking for answers.

Once the two left, Detective Abraham helped himself to a drink. As he sat he thought on ways he could have Ice-T murdered. His thoughts were quickly interrupted when he heard somebody knocking at his door. Detective Abraham looked through his peephole then opened the door.

"Hey, Detective," Serena said, standing outside of Detective Abraham's door. "May I come in?"

"Sure." Detective Abraham stepped to the side, so she could enter. "So what's on your mind?" He held out the Hennessy bottle toward her.

"No, thank you," Serena said politely.

"So how can I help you?"

"It's the money. These last three times I haven't been getting what me and Tone was supposed to get."

"We had to take a few losses," Detective Abraham said quickly. "We been having a few problems with a few people, but now we back on the right track."

"No disrespect, but that has nothing to do with me. Shit get messed up, you supposed to take the loss, never the connect."

"Listen, sweetie, you ain't the one out there in them streets, sweetheart, so don't come up in here with all that attitude."

"Ain't no attitude. I just want you to stick to the agreement and give me what you supposed to, or else I'm going to take my product and walk. Business is business."

Detective Abraham looked Serena up and down like she was beneath him. He yelled, "Don't walk up in here threatening me. Bitch, I told you shit was just a little fucked up, but we got shit back on track now!"

"Don't talk to me like that," Serena said, checking the detective. "Tone is your child, not me. All I want to know is, can I have the money you owe me?"

"I don't have it right now. I told you we had a little problem, but that's all taken care of now."

Serena could tell he was lying. She looked around and immediately got angry. Detective Abraham had a house full of new shit, but was playing games with her money. "You got my money or not?"

"I just told you, I don't have it."

"Fuck you then! You can kiss this good coke good-bye."

"Fuck you, bitch! You wasn't shit but an experiment anyway. The only reason Tone even talked to you in the first place was because I told him we knew all about you and your family's drug history. We used you!"

"You're a fuckin' liar. Tone isn't like that."

"You stupid bitch, we knew all about you and how your family don't deal with our kind. You were an experiment the whole time, so fuck you and your coke. You can shove it up your ass. I done already made enough money off you that I can retire."

"You're a fuckin' liar!" Serena cried as she turned and headed for the door.

"Whatever, bitch!" Detective Abraham yelled out. "Thanks for the money." He laughed as he watched Serena exit his home.

That can't be true, Serena thought to herself over and over again as she drove off and headed straight up to the jail. She had questions, and Tone was about to give her some answers.

Styles was cooking some Oodles & Oodles with tuna fish inside. "So what's the first thing you going to do when you get out?"

"Nigga, I'm going straight to Popeyes." Just thinking about their chicken brought a smile to Tone's face.

"I'm going straight to the soul food restaurant." Styles started busting down his Oodles & Oodles.

A C.O. walked up to their cell. "You got a visit," his voice boomed.

"Who?" Tone asked 'cause the C.O. didn't say a name.

"You!" the C.O. said, pointing at Tone.

"A'ight, give me a second." Tone threw on his State-green button-up shirt and brushed his waves. Then he gave Styles a pound. "Holla at you when I get back," he said, following the C.O. down to the visiting room.

Tone stepped foot in the visiting room and immediately spotted his baby. "Hey, baby," he said, his arms open for a hug.

"Sit down!" Serena growled.

"What's wrong?" Tone asked, helping himself to his seat.

Serena cut straight to the point. "Why did you start dealing with me?"

"What you mean, baby?" Tone said, a confused look on his face.

"Don't play stupid with me!" Serena yelled, getting stares from the other visitors.

"Were you only dealing with me 'cause you knew I had access to that butter?"

Tone looked over both shoulders. "Lower your voice. Are you gonna act like you got some sense, if I tell you the truth?"

"Just spit it out!"

"Okay, at first my father put me on you, hoping I could get access to that butter. But as soon as I got a chance to spend time with you, I knew you was the one for me."

Serena shook her head in disgust. "I look stupid to you?"

"Baby, I swear to you, I haven't touched another woman since I met you."

"I thought what we had was real." Serena looked at Tone like he had the mumps all over his face. "You just like the rest of these niggas out here!"

"That's bullshit, and you know it. I made a fuckin' mistake, and I really need you to forgive me."

"I can't." Serena stood to her feet. "You fucked everything up."

"Don't do this, baby. All I got is thirty days left until I get out. I need you to stay strong for your man."

"I can't do this anymore. Your father already told me everything, Tone, so you can save your lies." Serena turned and headed for the door.

As Serena exited the visiting room, Tone yelled at her back, "Thirty more days, baby!"

Chapter 17

Gruff slid out of his car and slowly crept up on the house he'd been watching for a week straight. He kicked open the back door and bum-rushed the crib. Inside he saw a house full of people sitting in the living room watching the Floyd Mayweather fight.

Gruff yelled, "Everybody on the floor now!" He popped a shot into the ceiling. *POW!*

He pulled out a roll of duct tape from his hoodie pocket and one by one taped the hands of every person in the crib.

He aimed his 9 mm at the head of the owner of the house. "Where the stash at?"

"Upstairs in the safe," the owner huffed, mad that he had been caught slipping.

"Don't give me no fuckin' attitude!" Gruff kicked the owner in his face.

Gruff headed upstairs to check out the safe. After he cleaned it out, he headed back downstairs and was stopped in mid-stride when he reached the living room.

"Don't take another step, fam!" a man wearing a ski mask barked, holding Gruff at gunpoint. "Drop that gun!"

"Listen, you don't know what you doing—"

POW! The gunman fired a round close to Gruff's head. "Nigga, I said drop the muthafuckin' gun!"

Gruff put the gun down, a smile on his face. "You making a mistake."

"I know," the gunman said in an uninterested tone. "Hand over that bag."

After Gruff tossed the bag at the gunman's feet, the gunman then picked up the duct tape and walked toward Gruff.

"Nah, you not taping me up," Gruff told him. "I got warrants. Take the money, but you not taping me up. You gon' have to shoot me before I go back to jail."

"Either get taped up or clapped up." The gunman looked at Gruff for an answer.

Gruff smirked. "Do what you gotta do."

POW! POW!

The gunman dropped Gruff with two shots to his chest. He then snatched the moneybag from off the floor. "Y'all have a nice day," he said, heading for the door.

"Don't move, muthafucka!" Gruff yelled from his knees as he aimed his other 9 at the gunman's back. "Drop the gun, and that money!" He winced in pain as he made his way over to the gunman.

The gunman quickly dropped both the gun and the moneybag.

Gruff picked up the moneybag then pressed his gun to the back of the gunman's head. "Let's go!" he ordered.

They hopped in the gunman's car.

"Drive!" Gruff said from the backseat, holding his chest.

"Where am I driving to?" the gunman asked.

"Your crib."

The gunman pulled up in front of his crib and let the engine die. "Man, is you gon' kill me or what?"

"Shut the fuck up and get out the car!"

Gruff escorted the gunman to his front door. "Nice-looking house you got here," Gruff said as they stepped inside.

He snatched off the gunman's ski mask and pushed him down on the couch. "You got two choices," Gruff began. "One, you die, or two, you become my partner, and we can get this money."

"Why would you want me to be partners with you after I just shot you?" the gunman asked.

"Because you got that fire inside of you, and I like how you just shoot instead of making empty threats." Gruff smiled as he peeled off his Kevlar bulletproof vest. "Plus, I need a nigga to watch my back, so a nigga like you can't never creep up on me. A nigga that ain't scared to let them thangs fly. So what's it going to be?" Gruff aimed his 9 mm at the gunman's head.

"Let's get this money," the gunman said with a smile.

"What's your name?" Gruff asked.

"Yayo."

"You got what it takes, kid," Gruff told him. "Stick with me and I'll take you straight to the top."

"Sorry for shooting you," Yayo said as he headed toward the kitchen to make himself a drink.

"You had to do what you had to do."

After Gruff had counted out the money he had just stole, he said, "Here," and tossed Yayo his half.

"Good looking," Yayo said, accepting the money.

"How did you know about that lick?"

"I been watching that house for the last two weeks," Yayo replied. "I saw you casing the joint for about a week. I would've been made my move, but I had to wait to see what you was going to do first." He paused. "I ain't know if you was a cop or what, know what I mean?"

"I feel you."

"So once I saw that you wasn't police, I made my move," Yayo said simply.

Gruff helped himself to a shot of Hennessy. "So who's next on your list?"

"Some cat named Ice-T."

"Ice-T?" Gruff repeated. "Never heard of him."

"Word?" Yayo said in disbelief. "Him and crew getting big money and I need in."

Gruff smiled. "If it makes dollars, then it always make sense."

"Fuck! Let's go get that money!" Yayo threw his shot back.

"Muthafuckas!" Maine growled as one of his soldiers pushed him out of the courtroom in his wheelchair out into the parking lot.

Detective Abraham sat in an all-black truck with tinted windows. He cracked the window before he spoke. "What it's looking like?"

"Them fuckin' crackers talking about seven years."

"Damn! Seven years for one gun?" Detective Abraham asked, making sure he heard right.

"Yeah, talking about, 'cause it had a silencer on it." A tear escaped Maine's eye. "I ain't going to be able to make it in jail for seven years in a fuckin' wheelchair!"

"Don't worry about no money," Detective Abraham said. "Whatever you need, I'll take care of it for you."

"I ain't worried about no money. I got four hundred grand stashed away in my crib. I can't do shit with that money in a fuckin' wheelchair."

"Everything going to be fine. Swing by my house later so we can talk," Detective Abraham said as he pulled off.

Maine sat in his wheelchair in the parking lot and just cried his eyes out.

***

"Today is the big day," Styles said with a smile as he watched Tone pack up his shit.

"I finally get my life back after three and a half years," Tone said. He was getting released early for good behavior.

"You still haven't heard from Serena?"

"Nah, she don't want nothing to do with me no more, and it's all my fault."

"You going to be all right," Styles said, trying to cheer up his friend. "At least you can talk to her now if you want, 'cause you on the outside. You can't do shit from in here."

"She probably done went back to Los Angeles. She ain't have no reason to stay up here, now that she ain't fuckin' with me."

"Keep your head up," Styles said, patting Tone on his back. "It ain't the end of the world."

"When you get up outta here, you better holla at me." Tone gave Styles a pound and a hug.

"Shit, I get out next month, so I'll be seeing you soon." Styles watched his friend and cell mate make his exit.

An hour later Tone was able to sign his release papers and walk out the front door. Tone was released with about thirteen other inmates. He stepped outside and saw some inmates kissing and hugging their loved ones. A few of them didn't have nobody to pick them up, and Tone fell into that pile.

Tone headed toward the bus station, which was only about three miles away. As he walked, he heard a car pull up behind him and beep the horn. He didn't look back, thinking it was for another inmate, but when the horn beeped again, he turned around and saw Serena stepping out of the driver's seat of the Range Rover, looking as sexy as ever. She ran up to Tone and jumped up on him, wrapping her arms around his neck and her legs around his waist.

"I missed you so much," she cried, as she held on as tight as she could.

"I love you, baby, and I promise it's just us from now on." Tone carried her back to the Range Rover and tongued her down.

"Promise you will never hurt me again."

"I promise you, baby."

Serena hopped back in the driver's seat. "Come on, let's get you as far away from this place as possible."

Two hours later Serena pulled up in the driveway of their crib, and that's when Tone saw the brand-new all-black 2011 Infiniti G35 coupe.

"Damn! That's for me?"

"Yup." Serena smiled. "My daddy's welcome-home gift."

As soon as Tone stepped foot in the crib, he went straight to the fridge and grabbed a bottle of wine, popped the cork and guzzled straight from the bottle. "Damn! That shit good!" Tone yelled like an animal.

"That taste good?"

"Hell yeah." Tone took another guzzle.

"I got something that taste better." Serena walked off, motioning with her finger for Tone to follow her.

Tone took about three more long swigs from the bottle before he headed back to the bedroom. When he got there, all Serena had on was a red thong to match her red fingernails and toenails.

"Damn! You so fuckin' sexy," Tone said through clenched teeth. He pulled Serena in close and tongued her down.

Serena moaned as she massaged Tone's dick through his jeans.

"Fuck this shit!" Tone quickly melted down to his knees and pushed Serena back on the bed. He quickly snatched her thong off. The first thing he did was gently kiss all over Serena's soaking-wet pussy. Tone then rubbed his face all in her juices before he went to work. He licked and sucked all over Serena's clitoris as he stuck two fingers inside of her walls.

"Ooooh shit!" Serena moaned as she squeezed on her titties, sucking on one of her nipples. "Damn, daddy! Eat your pussy!"

Tone moved his tongue like a rattlesnake, moving his head from side to side, as he sucked on Serena's pussy, forcing her to release in his mouth.

"You like how this pussy taste, daddy?"

Tone moaned, "Mmm-hmm."

"I need to feel that dick!" Serena pushed Tone's face away from her pussy and crawled up on the bed on all fours.

Tone wiped his mouth as he climbed up on the bed and slowly eased his way inside Serena's sopping wet pussy. At first he started off with slow, long strokes, but once he got into his rhythm, he sped up his strokes, pumping in and out of Serena with force and slapping her ass.

"You missed your daddy?"

"Yeees!" Serena groaned, throwing the pussy right back at him.

Tone tore the pussy up for about three more minutes, until he exploded inside of Serena.

"Oh my God," Serena said, catching her breath. "Damn! I forgot how good that dick was."

"Nah, I forgot how good my pussy was." Tone walked to the bathroom butt naked so he could take a shower.

After Tone got out the shower, he threw on one of his new outfits that Serena brought for him. As he heard her getting in the shower, he went back downstairs and grabbed his bottle of wine from off the counter and picked up where he left off.

Tone looked over at the door with his face crumpled up when he heard somebody knocking on it. He walked over to the door and snatched it open without looking through the peephole. On the other side of the door stood Young Mike and Harlem.

"I told you my man came home today," Young Mike said as he hugged Tone.

"My niggas, what's good?" Tone said, hugging both men.

"Came over here to see you," Harlem said with a smile.

Young Mike asked, "You seen your pops yet?"

"Nah, I'm not fuckin' with him no more. How he been treating y'all?"

"Paying us pennies," Young Mike replied. "Everything just went all downhill ever since you went away."

"Fuck that! I'm home now!" Tone said, giving both men dap. "I'm about to start up my own shit. Y'all niggas wanna be down?"

"What about your father?" Harlem asked.

"Fuck him! I'm going to see him tomorrow and let him know what I think of him and how he handles business."

"Hey, y'all." Serena waved as she came down the stairs and headed straight to the kitchen so she could start preparing a special dinner for her man.

"Fuck it!" Young Mike said. "If we can make some money, we both down."

"We definitely going to make some money." Tone smirked. "But, yo, I'ma holla at y'all tomorrow and run everything down to y'all, but right now y'all gotta get the fuck up outta here, so me and my baby can spend some much-needed time together."

"Handle your business." Young Mike smiled as he gave Tone a pound and made his exit.

Tone called out, "Yo, you got my house number, right?"

"Yeah, we got it." Harlem hopped in the passenger seat, and the truck pulled out of the driveway.

"Aww, baby, you could've talked to your friends for a little while, if you wanted to, while I cooked," Serena told him.

"I'll talk to them tomorrow." He guzzled from his bottle. "Tonight is all about you."

"No, tonight is all about *you*!" Serena corrected him.

An hour later Serena and Tone sat down and enjoyed Serena's cooking over a glass of wine. She cooked steak, mashed potatoes, and green beans.

"How does it taste, baby?"

"Delicious." Tone stuffed his face, eating as if he was still being timed.

"Damn! Slow down, daddy. Take a breath. You don't have to rush and eat, baby, you back home now."

"Sorry, but this my first real meal in almost four years."

"It's okay, daddy. Enjoy your food. That's why I made it." Serena sat back watching Tone, a smile on her face. Just having him back home was good enough for her.

Tone paused to sip on some wine. "So how niggas was treating you while I was away?"

"Like shit. They was playing games with the money the whole time, saying they was going to bring it one day then never show up."

"Did anybody ever disrespect you?"

"No, not really," Serena said, checking her memory. "Oh, every time Maine came to drop off the money, he would always have this look in his eyes."

"What kind of look?"

"The I-want-to-fuck-you kind of look."

"A'ight, this is the new plan." Tone changed the subject before he got too mad. "We about to set up our own shit, me, you, Harlem, Young Mike, and my man Styles. He's locked up right now, but he'll be out in about a month."

"How we going to do this?"

"We going to build this bitch from the ground up. From scratch."

"Whatever you need me to do, daddy, I got you." Serena pushed away from the table.

"Where you going?"

"I'm about to go slip into something a little more comfortable." Serena gave Tone a seductive look as she disappeared up the steps.

Tone sat at the table and finished off his second bottle of wine, just thinking about how the people closest to him shitted on him, and that a woman he had just met turned out to be more loyal. He just shook his head in disgust as he downed his last glass of wine.

Minutes later Serena returned back downstairs wearing black fishnet stockings that came up to her thick thighs, black boy shorts, and black pumps to match. Up top, she let her titties hang freely.

"Damn!" Tone said, admiring his woman's sexy features. He quickly stood, only to have Serena push him back down into the chair.

"Nigga, don't you move!" Serena squatted down and removed Tone's pants. His dick stood bobbing back and forth like a jack-in-the-box. Serena immediately grabbed his dick and began licking all over it like it was an icy, slobbing and spitting all over it the whole time, making loud moaning and slurping noises. "You like that, daddy?" she asked, jerking his dick, looking up in his eyes.

Before Tone could answer, she took his whole dick in her mouth again.

"Damn!" Tone groaned. He stood up and began fucking Serena's mouth like it was the last sexual encounter he would ever have in his life. He pulled Serena's hair as he began to speed up his strokes.

Serena gagged a little, but she kept on sucking like a pro, until Tone exploded in her mouth.

"Damn, baby!" an out-of-breath Tone said.

"Welcome home, daddy." Serena smiled as she wiped her mouth and headed back upstairs. "I ain't finished with you yet," she purred. "Follow me."

"Damn!" Tone wiped the sweat off his forehead as he followed Serena upstairs, where they had sex for the rest of the night.

The next morning Tone pulled up to his father's house bright and early. He slid out the new Infiniti and walked up to the front door.

Detective Abraham opened the door, a smile on his face. "So you just going to stand right there, or are you going to give your old man a hug?"

"What's up, Pops?" Tone said dryly, as he gave his father a hug.

"Look at what the cat just drug in," Detective Abraham announced.

Tone stepped in the living room and saw a bunch of new faces. The only one he recognized was Maine's, and he had to do a double-take when he saw him sitting in a wheelchair.

"Oooh shit! My nigga Tone. What's good?" Maine held out his hand for some dap, but Tone gave Maine a look of disgust as he ignored his extended hand.

"Glad to have you back home, son." Detective Abraham held out a drink for his son.

Tone smacked the drink out of his father's hand. "You's a grimy mufucka!" he yelled. "Stay the fuck away from me, and out of my life!" And he turned and headed for the door.

Before Tone could reach his car, Detective Abraham yelled, "Boy, what the fuck is wrong with you?"

"*You* are what's wrong with me," Tone huffed. "What happened to you holding me down while I was locked up?"

"I knew Serena was holding you down, so I fell back."

"So if you know she was holding me down, why the fuck you short her the money that was owed then tell her we was using her the whole time?"

"Shit got a little rough out here on the streets. You know how that shit go. You know what your problem is?"

"What?"

"You got business and pleasure mixed up." Detective Abraham smiled. "That bitch must be sucking your dick real good."

"What?" Tone said, his face crumpled up as he stole on his father.

Detective Abraham wasn't expecting the punch, so the impact caused him to backpedal a few steps. He wiped the blood from his mouth. "So you choosing that bitch over family?"

"What family?" Tone slid back in his Infiniti and pulled off.

Yayo and Gruff sat in the car across the street from the nice-looking hotel.

"Damn! This nigga need to hurry up," Yayo huffed.

"Patience, fam." Gruff blew out smoke from his cigarette.

A few minutes later, Gruff answered his ringing cell phone. "I'm listening," he answered.

"He just went up to his room," the desk clerk reported.

"A'ight. Good looking," Gruff hit the end button on his phone. "He just went up to his room."

Gruff and Yayo got out the car and headed inside the hotel.

"Damn, ma! Ya ass is looking mad fat," Nut said, as him and his lady friend hopped on the elevator full of white people and headed up to his room.

The whole ride to the hotel they'd both been telling each other how much they was going to put it on the other. As soon as Nut stepped foot in the room, he removed his gun and tossed it on the bed. Then he stripped down butt naked and lay across the bed. Tonya quickly followed his lead and stripped down to her birthday suit.

"Bring that fat ass over here!" Nut said, as he lay on the bed, stroking his dick with one hand.

"That's what you want?" Tonya asked in a sexually charged voice as she sat on Nut's face backwards and began clapping and jiggling her ass in his face. "You like that?" She leaned forward and placed Nut's dick in her mouth and sucked on it nice and slow, letting saliva drip all over the place.

Nut moaned and groaned as he sloppily sucked all over Tonya's clitoris, one finger stuck in her ass.

"Hi you doing today?" Gruff said politely to the desk clerk. He slipped her an envelope that held five hundred dollars inside.

The desk clerk handed Gruff the key to the room. "Room 404."

"Thanks." Gruff winked at the clerk as he headed over toward the steps. Him and Yayo reach the fourth floor then quickly caught their breath. "Damn! I gotta leave those Newports alone," Gruff said as they entered the hallway.

Once they reached the door, Yayo quickly threw on his ski mask.

"Fuck is that?" Gruff asked.

Yayo whispered, "I don't want the nigga to see my face."

"Let me find out these niggas got you shook." Gruff laughed as he slid the key in the slot.

As soon as the lock turned green, him and Yayo busted inside the room with their guns drawn. Inside the room Nut was sitting on a chair, while Tonya was bouncing up and down on his dick like she was trying to break it.

"Let me see them hands, fam!" Yayo yelled as he moved in close and pointed his .45 directly at Nut's head.

"Damn! Y'all could've at least waited until a nigga came first." Nut smirked, putting his hands up in the air.

The whole time Tonya continued to ride his dick.

"Bounce up and down one more time!" Gruff watched Tonya slowly ease up off Nut's equipment.

"What's this all about?" Nut asked.

"We know what you got in your trunk," Gruff said. "Just give us the keys, and we'll be on our way."

Yayo noticed Tonya looking over at Nut's gun over on the bed. "Bitch!" He swung his gun with all his might and hit her across the face, knocking her out instantly. He lifted up his foot and stomped her in her face for making him hurt his hand. "Muthafucka!"

Gruff smiled, looking at Nut. "Can we get those keys or what?"

"They right there in my pants pocket," Nut said, returning the smile.

Gruff walked over to his pants over in the corner on the floor.

Nut's dick immediately went down when he saw Gruff remove his keys from his pants pocket.

Once Gruff had the car keys, he removed a roll of duct tape from his back pocket. "Hands behind your back!" he ordered, and he taped up Nut's hands.

Then he tossed the tape to Yayo, so he could tape up Tonya's hands. After Yayo taped up Tonya's hands, they headed for the door.

"Hey!" Nut called out.

Gruff stopped at the door and looked in Nut's direction.

"I'ma see you later." Nut smirked.

"I'll be waiting." Gruff winked as he exited the room.

Gruff shot the desk clerk a wink as him and Yayo rushed out of the hotel.

They spotted Nut's Expedition about two blocks away.

Gruff opened up the back and removed the two duffel bags. He tossed one of them to Yayo, and the two headed back to their getaway car.

"What you about to get into?" Gruff asked, pulling out the parking spot.

"My girl coming through tonight," Yayo said, as he answered his ringing cell phone. "Hey, baby. What's up? . . . Damn! You there already? . . . A'ight, I'll be there in fifteen minutes."

Gruff pulled up on Yayo's block. "I'ma set up another lick for us tomorrow."

Yayo saw his girl sitting on the hood of her car, waiting for him. "Sound like a plan to me."

"That's your joint right there?" Gruff asked, nodding toward the girl sitting on the hood of the car.

"Yeah, that's all me." Yayo slid out the car. "You just keep your eyes on the road," he said playfully.

"Yo, grab one of those duffel bags. I'll keep one, just in case I don't make it home," Gruff said. "We'll split everything up tomorrow."

"A'ight, bet." Yayo gave Gruff some dap, grabbed the duffel bag from off the floor, and headed toward his crib. "Yo, come on!" he yelled over his shoulder.

Mary sucked her teeth. "Nigga, don't be rushing me, after I been here waiting on you for thirty minutes."

"You wasn't supposed to be here for another hour," Yayo said, opening up the front door.

"I was supposed to be meeting my brother to pick up some money." Mary kicked off her shoes. "But he ain't answering his phone."

"When am I going to meet this mystery brother of yours?" Yayo asked as he stripped down butt naked to get in the shower.

"Soon." Mary noticed that her man's hand was bleeding. "Baby, what happened to your hand? You're bleeding all over the carpet." She rushed to the bathroom, where she grabbed a washcloth, quickly wet it, and rushed back to the living room. "Here, put this on it," Mary said, wrapping the rag around Yayo's hand.

Yayo told her, "I had to knock this bitch the fuck out."

"Well, damn! How hard did you hit the bitch?"

"My hand is fine." Yayo snatched his hand away. "Let me hop in the shower real quick then you can bandage me up." He disappeared inside the bathroom, got in the shower, and stood directly under the shower.

Yayo favored the actor Mekhi Phifer, except that he had a little bit more muscles. He looked down at his hand and examined the nasty cut in the palm of his hand. Yayo stood in the shower caught up in a daydream when he felt a pair of hands grab his chest from behind.

"Damn, baby!" he said, wiping the water from his eyes. "You scared the shit outta me."

"I ain't going to hurt you, baby"—Mary turned Yayo around so he was facing her—"unless you want me to." She squatted down so she was face to face with Yayo's dick. She quickly slid his dick in her mouth and slurped all the water off of it, playing with her pussy with one hand and jerking his dick with the other hand.

Yayo guided her head with his hand. "Yeah, baby."

Mary pulled her head away quickly.

"What's wrong?" Yayo asked, a confused look on his face.

"I need my dick!" she said, rolling her eyes. "Last time I was sucking your dick, you came and left me hanging. We ain't doing that no more break me off and I'll break you off."

Mary turned around and bent over, placing her hands on the wall. A light moan escaped her lips when she felt Yayo enter her walls.

"Make sure you get all this pussy, baby." Mary spread one of her ass cheeks open, so Yayo could go up in her as far as possible.

Yayo watched as Mary's fat, juicy, wet ass cheeks clapped off his torso with each stroke he delivered.

After sliding in and out of Mary's wet walls for about fifteen minutes, he quickly pulled out and watched his semen flow down the drain with the rest of the water.

Once they was out the shower, Mary wrapped up Yayo's hand as the two lay in bed watching re-runs of *The Fresh Prince*, until they both fell asleep.

"Fuck it! Why not?" Gruff said to himself as he pulled into the parking spot in front of the bar. For some reason he just didn't feel like going straight to his run-down roach-motel room tonight. He walked up in the bar and quickly found a table over in the corner.

A waitress came over. "How you doing tonight, sir?" she said politely. "My name is Denise. Can I get anything for you tonight?"

"Yeah, let me get a bottle of Cîroc and a bottle of orange juice." Gruff pulled out a big wad of cash. "How much?"

"Your total is one seventy," Denise said, looking Gruff in his eyes.

"Here you go, ma." He handed her two hundred-dollar bills. "Keep the change."

"Thanks, sweetie." Denise winked as she walked off to go cover his order.

Once the waitress walked off, Gruff quickly scanned the whole place. He noticed a few jump-offs giving him the eye over at the bar.

Denise came back with his bottle of Cîroc and orange juice. "I get off in ten minutes. You better save me a drink." She smiled as she walked off.

"I got you!" Gruff yelled loud enough so that she could hear him. He craned his neck so he could get a better look at Denise's ass. She had a nice-sized ass for a "slim goody." *Yeah, I might have to take that down tonight.* Gruff smirked as he bobbed his head to the sound of Young Jeezy's voice blaring throughout the bar.

Ten minutes later Denise returned to Gruff's table as promised. "You got that drink for me?" she asked, looking down at Gruff.

Gruff nodded toward the bottle. "Help yourself."

Denise poured herself a drink and quickly sipped it. "May I have a seat?"

"Of course." Gruff tried to look at her ass from the front.

"So, you live around here?"

"Why?" Gruff asked defensively.

"Because I been working here for two years and this is my first time seeing you come in here."

Gruff lied, "Nah, I live in Harlem."

"So what you doing all the way out in Brooklyn at this time of night?"

"Just came to get my drink on?"

"What's your name?"

"Mr. Perfect." Gruff smiled.

"Mr. Perfect, huh?" Denise laughed. "If it works for you, then it works for me."

"What you doing later?"

"I'm about to go home."

"You want some company?"

"I wish." Denise laughed. "I live with my man, and he don't play that shit. He's on his way up here to pick me up now."

"Oh so that's why you keep on looking at your cell phone?" Gruff sipped on his drink.

"Yeah, he's going to call me when he's outside."

"Let me get your number before you disappear on me," Gruff said smoothly.

"Are you crazy? I'm not giving you my number! But I'll take yours."

Gruff smiled as he jotted his number down on a napkin and slid it over to her. "Make sure you call me too."

"I got you, Mr. Perfect." She smiled as she slid the napkin inside of her purse. "Can I get another drink before I go?"

"Help yourself." Gruff nodded toward the bottle once again.

Denise smiled as she grabbed the bottle and poured herself another drink.

A deep voice boomed, "DENISE!!!!"

Denise's whole body jumped when she heard that voice. "Umm, hey, Rah Rah." She got up and moved in for a hug.

Rah Rah declined her hug. He yelled, "Fuck is you over here doing?"

"Nothing. I was just talking and having a drink. Why you tripping?" Denise asked, trying to hide the fear in her voice.

Rah Rah growled, "I look stupid to you, bitch?" He smacked the shit out of Denise in front of everybody. Then he locked his eyes on Gruff. "And who the fuck is this chump?"

"He ain't nobody," Denise said, praying nothing popped off. "He just offered me a drink."

"Fuck is you out drinking with this chump for?" Rah Rah yelled. "If you wanna drink then you bring ya ass home and drink!"

"Chump?" Gruff echoed, standing to his feet. "Fuck is you calling a chump?"

"Let's go home, baby," Denise said, jumping in front of Rah Rah.

"Bitch, get the fuck out my way!" Rah Rah shoved Denise down to the floor.

The owner of the bar quickly jumped in. "Hey," he yelled, "if y'all fools wanna fight, take that shit outside!"

"Let's take this shit outside," Rah Rah growled, leading the way outside.

Gruff gripped his 9 mm as he walked up out the bar.

"What's popping?" Rah Rah yelled like he was on steroids as he threw hands up in a fighting stance.

Gruff smirked as he stuck his 9 mm back in its holster and walked off toward his car.

"Yeah, that's what I thought!" Rah Rah yelled. "You better walk away, you punk-ass bitch!"

Gruff slid in his car and just pulled off.

Chapter 18

Tone pulled up in front of Mya's house and let the engine die. He walked up to the front door and knocked on it. Mya answered the door, still looking as sexy and beautiful as ever.

"Hey, Tone," she sang as she gave him a hug. "Glad you made it home in one piece."

"Why you ain't never bring my son up there to see me?" Tone said, getting straight to the point.

"Maybe because I didn't want him to see you caged up like some animal."

"Whatever! Can I see my son now?"

"He's asleep," Mya said quickly.

"Well, can I at least see him?"

"You going to have to come back tomorrow."

"For what?"

Mya raised her voice. "Because it's late. That's why!"

"My son is about to be four years old, and I haven't even seen him yet. What the fuck!"

"Like I said, come back tomorrow and you can see him."

A voice from the background yelled, "Yo, who the fuck is that at the door?"

"It's nobody," Mya replied, trying to shut the door.

A man with long dreadlocks and a body full of tattoos came to the door wearing nothing but a pair of boxers. He pushed Mya out the way. "Can I help you, fam?"

"Yeah, I'm here to see my son."

"You don't think it's kind of late to be coming by?" Dread asked.

"Listen, I just got out of jail and ain't seen my son since he was born. Can I please just see him?" Tone was running out of patience.

"You see, I was going to let you see him, but I don't think I like your attitude."

Tone pulled out his .45 and stuck it under the Dread's chin and backed him inside the house. "Nigga," he yelled, "I paid for this mu'fuckin' house! You don't tell me when I can see my son!"

"Why don't you put that gun down and fight me like a man! You real tough with that gun in your hand."

"Shut the fuck up!" Tone grabbed Dread by his hair and slammed him down to the floor.

Before Tone could turn around, Mya had shattered a wine bottle over his head.

Tone stumbled into the wall but kept his footing. He immediately aimed his .45 at Mya's head. And Mya closed her eyes and braced herself for the shot that never came.

"Bitch, get on the fuckin' floor!" Tone barked, holding the top of his bloody head.

Mya quickly did as she was told.

Once both of them was on the floor, Tone quickly dipped in his son's bedroom and flicked on the light. His son lay in the bed sleeping peacefully. Tone walked over and kissed him on the cheek before exiting the room. Then he walked straight past Mya and her new boyfriend and walked out the front door.

Serena was sitting on the couch in the living room wearing a wifebeater and some boy shorts, when Tone walked through the front door with his head all bloody.

"Oh my God!" Serena screamed, jumping to her feet. "What happened to your head?"

"I went over to Mya's crib to go see my son and got into it with her and her new man."

"So what happened to your head, baby?" Serena asked as she put his head in the tub under the faucet.

"That bitch Mya busted me over the head with a bottle." Tone winced as the water ran over his cut.

Once the cut was cleaned, Serena wrapped his head up to stop the bleeding. "You a'ight?"

"Yeah, I'm fine," Tone replied, flopping down on the couch.

"Here." Serena tossed a duffel bag on Tone's lap. "I went and picked that up today."

Tone peeked inside the duffel bag and saw ten white bricks sitting in the bag. "A'ight. I'ma get on the grind tomorrow."

"Did you go see your parole officer yet?"

"Yeah, I seen her earlier today." Tone shook his head. "Bitch talking about, I got a nine o'clock curfew."

"Nine o'clock? Damn! What's that all about?"

Tone shrugged his shoulders. "I need you to do me a favor."

"What's up?"

"I need you to come over here, take off them boy shorts, and bend over. Now!"

"Okay, daddy." Serena smiled as she did as she was told. She quickly removed her boy shorts and bent all the way over, grabbing her ankles.

Tone smoothly sat up straight on the couch and began kissing all over Serena's ass. He then slid a little lower and sucked on her clitoris from behind.

"Awww yeah, daddy! Eat this pussy!" Serena moaned, looking back at her man. "Yeah, daddy, just like that!" she yelled as she released in his mouth.

Tone sucked on her pussy like he was an animal, not even coming up for air. Serena came three times before he finally stopped.

"Oh my God!" Serena said, out of breath.

Tone stood up and slipped the head inside her wet pussy. "Grab them ankles for your daddy."

He slid in and out her at a rapid pace until he came all up inside of her. "Ooooh shit!" Tone exhaled as he lay stretched out on the floor right next to Serena, where the two slept for the rest of the night.

Gruff sat parked over in the cut, his eyes glued to the front of the bar. In the passenger seat sat Tiger, who Gruff purposely didn't feed for three days.

"You about to eat in a minute." Gruff rubbed on Tiger's fur as he looked at his watch.

Moments later Gruff saw Rah Rah pull up and enter the bar.

"Come, girl, let's go." Gruff and Tiger slid out the car and walked over to Rah Rah's truck.

"Come on. Why every time I come up in here you got me waiting and shit?" Rah Rah asked. "Why you ain't never ready?"

"Sorry," Denise said, trying her hardest to tune the big man out. "I'm ready right now."

"About damn time!"

When Rah Rah and Denise exited the bar, Rah Rah saw the guy he was going to pound out a week ago sitting on the hood of his truck.

Rah Rah growled, "Oh, this nigga must want to die!" He removed his watch and bracelet. He stopped dead in his tracks when he saw he saw the vicious-looking pit bull sitting on her hind legs, looking him dead in his eyes.

Gruff smirked as he took another pull from his cigarette. "Sic him!"

Rah Rah quickly took off back in the direction of the bar, but he didn't get far. Tiger jumped up and dragged him down to the floor by his arm.

"Oh my God! Somebody help!" Denise screamed out in horror.

Gruff quickly pulled out his 9 mm and shot Denise in the neck, shutting her the fuck up. He looked over and saw Tiger had a tight grip on Rah Rah's neck. "Come on, let's go!" he yelled.

Tiger ran back to the car, and Gruff peeled out of the parking lot, leaving tire marks all over the place.

Serena pulled up in front of Mya's salon and marched straight into her shop. "Bitch, bring your ass outside!" she barked.

"Don't come up in here with all that noise," Mya countered.

"I don't wanna talk. I came here to get busy" Serena said inviting Mya outside again.

"What's this all about?" Mya asked, putting her hair in a ponytail.

"Bitch, keep your hands off my man!"

"Well, keep your man away from my house at wee hours of the night."

"Bitch, just come outside," Serena said, leading the way outside.

A few of Mya's employees tried to stop her from going outside, but Mya didn't pay them any mind as she stepped outside. Deep down she was still heated that Serena had stole her man.

As soon as Mya stepped outside, Serena was all over her, swinging with bad intentions. The two women got a hold of one another's hair and went to work on each other, neither one holding back. They went at it blow for blow until the cops came and separated them.

"Bitch, stay the fuck away from my man!" Serena yelled as an officer threw her in the back of one of the squad cars.

"Fuck you and your man, bitch!" Mya yelled, as she too got placed in the back of one of the police cars.

Tone sat at the kitchen table along with Young Mike and Harlem. In the middle of the table sat a brick.

"I'ma need y'all to go hard out here in these streets," Tone told them. "We the only ones out here with this product. Get y'all a team together and make it do what it do."

"So you cut your pops off for good?" Young Mike asked.

"For good. He a grimy muthafucka and not a man of his word."

"I feel you on that one," Harlem cut in. "'Cause the nigga even started shorting me and Young Mike too."

"It's a new day," Tone said. "And everybody is going to eat." He answered his ringing cell phone. "Who this?"

"Baby, it's me," Serena said.

"No number came up when you called."

"Because I'm in jail."

"In jail?" Tone repeated. "What you doing in jail?"

"I went and fucked that bitch Mya up."

"Why, baby? I told you to leave that shit alone."

"You must be crazy. Ain't no bitch busting my man in the head with a bottle and getting away with it."

Tone just shook his head. "What that bail looking like?"

"Twenty thousand."

"A'ight, I gotta go take care of something, so I'ma have Young Mike come through and pick you up. That's cool?"

"I don't care, as long as I get out of here."

"A'ight, sit tight. Help is on the way," Tone said, ending the conversation. He turned to Young Mike. "I need you to do me a favor 'cause I gotta run out real quick."

"I got you. Just let me know what you need me to do," Young Mike replied.

Tone ran everything down to Young Mike, handed Harlem the brick, and minutes later the trio went their separate ways.

"So you saying the nigga that robbed you didn't even wear a mask?" Ice-T laughed.

"That shit not funny," Nut said seriously. "That nigga took the whole re-up."

"I know," Ice-T said. "We gon' catch him."

"So what we going to do about getting some more work?" Nut asked.

"I guess I'ma have to come out the pocket, since we took such a loss. But I need you and the rest of the soldiers out hunting this stickup kid, 'cause I don't play that robbery shit."

Nut told him, "You know I'ma catch that nigga."

"Look at this nigga." Ice-T pointed to the monitor that showed the front, back, and sides of his house. Him and Nut watched as Tone pulled up and eased out of his car headed toward the front door.

Nut and a few other soldiers went outside to meet Tone. "This nigga must be crazy!" Nut blocked Tone's path. "You lost or something?"

"I didn't come here for no trouble," Tone said. "I just need to speak to Ice-T."

"I should pop ya head off right now for even having the nerve to come up here!" Nut pulled out his .38.

"I just need to speak to Ice-T," Tone repeated.

"Nigga, we don't talk to the muthafuckin' police!" Nut yelled.

Just as Nut was about to pistol-whip Tone, Ice-T stepped out on the porch. "Fuck you want?"

"I need to holla at you," Tone said.

"About what?"

"Business."

"This better not be no bullshit."

"Trust me, it's not," Tone assured him.

"Follow me." Ice-T escorted him inside the crib. "You want a drink?"

"Yeah, I'll take some Grey Goose and orange juice." Tone helped himself to a seat.

Ice-T handed Tone his drink. "So what's on your mind?"

Tone sipped his drink. "You wanna make some money?"

"Hell yeah. Now what's up?"

"I can guarantee you the best product out here on the streets, if you can guarantee me your loyalty."

"Fuck is you talking about? Where you get work from?" Ice-T asked suspiciously.

Tone smiled, knowing he was the only with access to that pure uncut shit. "I got the plug."

"I heard your pops had some pure shit on his hands too."

"Nah, that was all me, but I don't fuck with my pops no more. But I still have to get rid of the shit, and that's where you come in at."

"How I know I can trust this shit?"

"Listen, I just came home and I need to stack up some paper, and I ain't got time to be playing no games. You got my word."

"Your word better be bond!" Ice-T said. "How soon can you get them thangs to me?"

"I got nine of them bitches in my trunk right now."

"Word?" Ice-T said, excited. "Fuck it! give me all nine. Them shits better be official too."

"Once I see that paper, I got you."

"A'ight, give me a second." Ice-T disappeared up the stairs. He returned ten minutes later with a duffel bag. "Here," he said, sitting the duffel bag on the table.

Tone quickly thumbed through the cash. "Look straight." He stood and picked up the bag.

"You buggin'," Ice-T said quickly. "That money ain't going nowhere until I test each one of them thangs."

"No problem. Give me a second."

Tone stepped outside and headed to the car. He looked over both shoulders before removing the duffel bag from his trunk and returning back inside Ice-T's crib.

"That's for you." Tone smiled as he sat the duffel bag on the table right next to the other duffel bag.

Ice-T took his time checking each joint, making sure everything was proper. "And you said you can get more of this?"

"Ten at a time," Tone answered.

"Bet. I'ma need ten more of these bitches in about four days."

"Here's my number." Tone punched it inside Ice-T's cell phone. "I deal with you direct and only you."

"You got it," Ice-T said, as he walked Tone to the door. He stopped Tone before he stepped out the house. "Let me ask you question—Would you have any hard feelings if I had your father murdered?"

"What father?"

Tone exited Ice-T's house and headed to his car. He popped the trunk, tossed the duffel bag in the trunk, and drove off.

When Tone drove off, Nut asked, "Fuck was that shit all about?"

"This nigga might be our ticket out of the game," Ice-T said. "I don't know where he getting it from, but he got his hands on some good shit."

"Where he get it from?" Nut asked.

"I have no idea."

"You think this shit is a setup?" Nut asked, eyebrow raised.

"Nah, I don't get that feeling from him." Ice-T finished off his drink. "He ain't never been that type of nigga."

"I hope not."

Just then a young worker ran up in the crib.

"What up, little nigga?"

"Just got word on that stickup kid," the young worker said, out of breath. "His name is Gruff, and he lives in Brooklyn somewhere. He the one who shot up Maine and put him in a wheelchair."

"I heard of that nigga." Ice-T poured himself another drink. "A real nothing-to-live-for-ass nigga."

"I'ma track that ass down," Nut said seriously.

"Everybody talking about how his dog be eating niggas alive and shit," the young worker reported.

"Yeah, I'ma find him before the week is out. Good looking." Nut handed the young worker a few bills.

Ice-T smiled as he gave Nut a pound. "Time for you to go hunting."

Chapter 19

Serena walked in the house and sat the duffel bag on the table. "Ten more," she announced.

"Good job, baby," Tone said as he sat at the kitchen table counting money.

Serena kissed Tone on his lips. "Damn! Do you got enough rubber bands?"

"You can never have enough rubber bands." Tone took a swig from his bottle of Henny. "How did everything go?"

"Smooth as usual," Serena said, kicking off her shoes. "I didn't check 'em out though." She pulled them out the duffel bag, and they both examined them.

Tone held one up. "They look straight to me."

A loud knock at the door caused the two of them to jump.

"Who the fuck is that?" Serena whispered.

"I don't know," Tone whispered. "Pack all this shit up." He grabbed his .45 from off the counter and eased his way toward the door. He looked through the peephole and saw his parole officer standing on the other side of the door. "Shit! it's my parole officer!" Tone stuck his gun in the duffel bag, and Serena ran upstairs to go hide it. Once Serena was upstairs, he opened the door. "What's up, Ms. Johnson?" He stepped to the side so she could enter.

"How are you?" Ms. Johnson asked, looking around.

"Everything is cool," Tone replied nervously.

"Why are you sweating?"

"Oh, I just got finished doing some push-ups," he lied.

"Did you find yourself a job yet?"

"Not yet. I'm still looking. Shit hard out here."

"Okay, if you don't find anything within the next thirty days, I'm going to have to assign something for you, unless you get in school."

"I'll have something before thirty days." Tone smiled.

"Okay, I'll see you in two weeks at my office." Ms. Johnson shook Tone's hand then made her exit.

Serena peeked her head down the steps. "She gone?"

"Yeah, she gone." Tone wiped the sweat from his forehead. "We gotta find a place to keep all this shit tomorrow."

"Okay, baby, I'm about to hop in the shower real quick." Serena disappeared back up the steps.

Tone just threw on an old Jay-Z CD and sipped on his Henny as he sat in deep thought until it was time for him to go to bed.

Gorilla Zoe's song, "Hood Nigga," blared through the speakers in Yayo's crib as Mary stood up on the coffee table wearing nothing but an orange thong and some orange pumps, shaking her ass for her man.

"Shake that shit, baby," Yayo said as he playfully tossed a few singles up in the air.

"You like that?" Mary looked back at Yayo and made each one of her ass cheeks bounce one at a time in a nice speed.

"Where the fuck did you learn how to do that at?"

"Don't worry about all that." Mary began making her ass clap.

Yayo felt his cell phone vibrating on his hip, and he quickly answered. "Yo."

"Where you at?" Gruff asked.

"In the crib. Why? What's up?"

"I'm right outside. I got a lick for us. Don't have me waiting out here for a long time," Gruff said, ending the call.

Yayo pressed mute on the remote to his sound system.

"Oh hell no!" Mary huffed. "You ain't going nowhere right now!"

"Baby, I'll be back in fifteen minutes tops." Yayo ran upstairs and grabbed his ski mask and an extra click for his .45.

"I love you, baby. I'll be back in a few."

"Take all the time you want. I'll be 'sleep by the time you get back." Mary kicked off her orange heels and stomped all the way upstairs.

"I love you!" Yayo yelled as he slipped out the front and hopped in the car that awaited him.

"Took you long enough," Gruff joked as he pulled off.

"So what we about to get into?" Yayo asked, checking the magazine in his .45.

"Some punk-ass Mexicans supposed to be dropping off mad pounds of weed tonight at this motel around the corner. This going to be a easy night tonight."

"I hope so."

An hour after they'd pulled up into the motel's parking lot, Gruff and Yayo noticed two cars pull up side by side. One of the drivers grabbed a big rolling suitcase from out of his trunk, while the other only removed a duffel bag from his backseat. Both drivers looked nervous and suspicious, like they was up to no good.

"I'ma kick in the door," Gruff said, cracking his neck. "If any one of those taco-eating muthafuckas act up, you know what to do."

Yayo nodded his head as he slipped on his ski mask.

"What's up with you and that damn ski mask?" Gruff asked, his face crumpled up.

"What you mean?" Yayo asked. "I don't want mutha-fuckas I rob to see my face."

"That's the whole thrill of it, letting a muthafucka know that it was you who robbed him." Gruff smiled.

"Nah, you bugging."

Yayo and Gruff slid out the car and slowly crept up to the room door they were looking for.

On the silent count of three, Gruff came forward and kicked open the door.

"Let me see them hands!" Gruff forcefully slammed one of the Mexicans down to the floor.

Yayo, smiling from behind his ski mask, had his .45 aimed at the other Mexican's head.

"Hold me down." Gruff removed a roll of duct tape from his back pocket. He quickly taped one of the Mexican's hands up before moving on to the next one.

Yayo quickly grabbed the suitcase and rushed out the door. Gruff grabbed the duffel bag from off the floor and followed Yayo's lead.

Once back in the car, Gruff put the pedal to the metal and jetted up out the parking lot.

"That's some good shit you got." Ice-T laughed as him and Tone traded duffel bags.

"I told you I had it," Tone boasted. "Straight off the boat."

"We going out tonight. You wanna roll?"

"Yeah, my man come home today," Tone suddenly remembered. "So I think we might take you up on that offer."

"Good," Ice-T said. "Go out and celebrate our new success."

Nut came running down the stairs. "Just got word on where that nigga Gruff rest his head." He smiled as he headed out the door.

"That nigga Gruff is a pain in the ass," Tone said.

Ice-T shook his head. "Tell me about it."

"Let me get up outta here." Tone stood up to leave. "I'ma get with you later on."

"Do that." Ice-T gave Tone a pound as he walked out the door.

Tone walked in the door and dropped the duffel bag on Serena's lap. "We need another order."

"Damn! Already?" Serena said with a smile on her face. "That Ice-T nigga ain't playing."

"I need you to do me a favor." Tone pulled a stack of money from out of his pocket and tossed it to her. "Go get yourself a nice outfit. We going out tonight."

"A club or dinner?"

"Club. My man Styles should be here any minute."

"Oh, that's why you rushing me?" Serena joked.

"No. I'm rushing you 'cause I know you going to take all day." Tone playfully mushed Serena.

"Okay, okay." Serena laughed.

Just then she heard somebody knocking. She answered the door with a smile, extending her hand. "You must be Styles."

"And you must be the Serena I've heard so much about," Styles countered.

"That would be me." Serena stepped to the side so he could enter.

Tone smiled as he gave Styles a pound followed by a hug. "So I see you finally made it home."

"Finally." Styles smiled.

"I'll see you later, baby." Serena kissed Tone on his lips as she slipped out the door.

"So what's planned for tonight?" Styles sat at the bar area.

Tone poured him and Styles a drink. "Suppose to be this big-ass party going down tonight."

"As long as it's going to be some hos there, I'm cool." Styles downed his drink in one gulp. It had been years since he had been with a woman, and he couldn't wait to get back into the loop.

"Definitely gonna be some nice pieces up in there."

"If the ass is round, you know I'm down." Styles smiled.

Nut sat parked across the street from a run-down motel along with three youngblood niggas. "Yo, you sure this the raggedy motel this clown is staying at?"

A young shooter with a red flag tied around his head answered, "Yeah," from the backseat.

After waiting for about two hours, Nut spotted Gruff. "There that nigga go right there," he said, looking at the man walk his dog.

"You want us to air that nigga out?" the young shooter asked.

"Nah, not yet," Nut said, watching Gruff closely. "I need to know a little more about him. Plus, it's a precinct right around the corner. We gon' watch this clown for about a week then go from there."

Ice-T's Range Rover pulled up in the club's parking lot bumping Gucci Mane's new CD. He slid out the passenger side of the truck looking like a million bucks. He wore all black—black jeans, yellow construction Tims, a black long john shirt, some black shades, and a black skully hat sat tilted to the side of his head. The two white gold chains and the iced-out pinky ring and bracelet just added to his look.

"I hope it ain't no dickhead at the door," Ice-T said out loud as he led the way toward the entrance.

"Whooooa!" the bouncer said, holding out his arm. "I'ma need to see some ID, fellas."

"Stop playing all the time." Ice-T gave the bouncer a pound. "They all with me."

"No problem." The bouncer laughed as he let Ice-T and his whole crew in.

Another big bouncer quickly escorted Ice-T to the VIP booth, knowing the crew was about to spend some real money in the club tonight. Remy Ma's song, "Conceited," came blaring through the speakers, and all the chicks in the club started going crazy.

A lady came carrying a bucket full of ice and four bottles of Grey Goose sticking out of it.

"Now we can really get this party started." Nut poured himself a drink.

Once Ice-T saw Nut drinking the Grey Goose straight, he knew he was going to fuck around and get into some shit tonight, but he ignored his friend and tried to focus on having a good time.

"Damn!" Nut said, looking down at the ass of the freak he was dancing with. He grabbed her waist with one hand and held his bottle up in the air with the other as the two flowed to the beat.

Tone stepped out the Infiniti looking regular. He wore a tan Dickies suit, some all-black suede Tims, and a black White Sox fitted hat pulled down low. The only jewelry he wore was an iced-out bracelet, a watch, and a diamond-flooded pinky ring.

Serena, on the other hand looked, brand new. She wore this tight-fitting all-white tube dress that stopped at the middle of her thighs. She completed her outfit with some red heels, and she wore her hair up in a lazy bun, the bright red clip in her hair matching her shoes. On her neck she wore a diamond-studded chain, on her wrist sat a white gold bracelet that spelled Tone's name in diamonds, and on her ring finger was her new engagement ring that Tone had given her earlier that night.

In the background stood Young Mike, Harlem, and Styles.

"Everybody good?" Tone asked.

"We good," Young Mike replied, tossing a piece of gum in his mouth.

After twenty minutes of arguing with the bouncer, Tone and his crew was allowed to enter. Tone stepped foot in the club, and immediately the heat, bright lights, and pumping bass slapped him in the face. Lil Wayne and Birdman's song, "Always Strapped," had the club jumping. He looked over the crowd and saw Ice-T and his crew up in the VIP section.

"Come on, baby!" Tone yelled over the loud music. He grabbed Serena's hand, and the two knifed their way through the crowd.

A light-skinned cat with waves grabbed Serena's wrist. "Damn, ma!" he yelled over the music. "You gorgeous!"

Serena quickly snatched her wrist away before Tone could see what was going on.

Tone reached the VIP and tried to brush past the bouncer. "Yo, that's my peoples up in there."

The big sweaty bouncer blocked the entrance and looked at Tone like he was lying. "C'mon, son!"

Tone quickly smacked the bouncer's sweaty paw from off his chest. "Yo, my man, don't put ya fuckin' hands on me!"

Nut reached down over the rail and tapped the bouncer on his shoulder. "Let him up here," he yelled over the music. "He's with us!"

Tone grilled the bouncer as him and Serena walked past him up into the VIP section. Tone looked behind him and noticed that only Young Mike was behind him. Harlem and Styles had disappeared somewhere in the crowd.

When Young Mike locked eyes with Nut, the two didn't speak, thinking back on the time when their crews had clashed in the club.

"Glad you could make it." Ice-T gave Tone and Young Mike a pound. He turned to Serena and gave her a head nod.

By this time the VIP section was filled with partygoers. Serena sat on the sideline sipping on some wine, while Tone stood talking to Ice-T.

"I'm feeling this party," Tone commented.

"This everyday shit." Ice-T shrugged his shoulders. "Get used to this."

"I think I can get used to this." Tone sipped on his drink.

A light-skinned girl walked up to Tone. "Hey, what's up? You from Cali or something?" The girl nodded toward his Dickies suit.

Tone chuckled. "Nah, I'm not from Cali."

"What's with the Dickies suit then?"

"Just what I feel comfortable in." While serving time, Tone had got used to rocking Dickies suits.

"Oh. Well, it does look good on you," she said. "Can you get me a drink?"

"Yeah, the bottles are right there. Help yourself." Tone pointed toward the bottles.

"Can you get it for me? I don't wanna just go over there grabbing people's bottles and shit."

"Chill. You wildin'. My girl sitting right over there." Tone nodded in Serena's direction. "You trying to get me in trouble?"

"Oh, that's your girl right there?" Light-skin looked over at Serena and rolled her eyes. "Oh, my bad. I ain't know it was like that." Light-skin walked off.

As soon as Tone turned around, Serena motioned for him to come.

"You wanna get fucked up?" she said over the music in a way only he could hear her.

"Why? What happened?" Tone said, playing dumb.

"Don't play with me," Serena told him. "Keep them bitches out your face!"

"Sorry, baby. It won't happen again."

Just then Tone saw Styles enter the VIP section. "I thought you got lost for a second," he said, giving Styles a pound.

"Yo, I just saw that box-head nigga that we fucked up while we was behind the wall," Styles said excitedly.

"Word?" Tone asked.

"Nigga up in here mad deep," Styles informed him. "Nigga saw me and started whispering and pointing at me like they was plotting on me."

"Don't worry about it. Everything is going to be cool."

Tone was wishing he could take back his words when he saw Box Head and his crew headed for their VIP section. Box Head, whose name was Gary, stomped up into the VIP section with the rest of his crew like he owned it.

"Thought you wasn't never going to see me again, right? You little bitch!" Gary huffed all up in Tone's face, his breath smelling like tacos and ass.

"Yo, fam, check this out," Tone began, "me and my peoples ain't here for all that. We here to have a good time. Leave that jail shit back in jail."

"Fuck you and your peoples, muthafucka!" Gary said, letting spittle fly on Tone's face.

Tone sighed loudly as he turned and quickly punched Gary in the face, sending him stumbling back into his peoples. Once that happened, all hell broke loose.

Ice-T looked over and saw Tone getting it on with about twenty niggas. He quickly jumped into the fight, followed by Nut and all the blood niggas he came with.

Next thing you know, a "Royal Rumble" broke out in the VIP section. Ladies were being pushed down to the floor, and drinks were spilling all over the place as the brawl spread out onto the dance floor.

Twenty minutes later the bouncers finally gained control of the situation.

"Baby, are you okay?" Serena asked when she saw that the cut on Tone's head had been reopened.

"Yeah, I'm fine. Let's get up outta here." He grabbed her hand and made a beeline for the exit.

Once they got outside, it sounded like Vietnam. Nut and his blood homies were having a shootout in the parking lot with Gary and his crew.

"Come on, let's get outta here!" Tone said, and him and Serena hopped in the Infiniti. Tone backed out of his parking spot and left the whole parking lot smelling like burnt rubber.

"You heard about that bitch-ass nigga, Tone?" Maine took a swig from his E & J.

"Nah. What's up with that scumbag?" Detective Abraham asked.

"Nigga blowing up out here on these streets with that coke connect." Maine took another swig. "He even hooked up with Ice-T."

"Get the fuck outta here," Detective Abraham said in disbelief. "He wouldn't do no shit like that, knowing me and Ice-T got beef."

"If I'm lying, I'm dying. It ain't no secret. Everybody know."

"That grimy, little, sneaky muthafucka!" Detective Abraham growled. "I'ma teach his ass about playing with grown folks."

Maine knew that look on Detective Abraham's face. "What you gonna do?"

"Ever since that bitch came into the picture, she been messing everything up. She done even turned my son against me. But now it's her time to go."

"You going to kill her?" Maine asked with a smile on his face.

"Nah," Detective Abraham answered quickly. "I'm going to put her ass in jail." He laughed just at the thought of it.

"Damn! You cold-blooded." Maine chuckled. "But—fuck it!—you gotta do what you gotta do."

"You muthafuckin' right."

Mary knocked on the door with force. "Making me come over here all early and shit," she mumbled to herself as she knocked again.

Nut snatched open the door. "Fuck is you banging like the police for?"

"Nigga, you the one who called me over here at eight o'clock in the morning." Mary brushed past her brother. "Now what's up? 'Cause a bitch is tired."

"I need your help," Nut told her. "I need to use you as bait to catch this nigga who robbed me."

"Nah, I'm not doing all that. Next thing you know, I'ma fuck around and get shot again. Nah, I'm not doing it."

"You not going to get shot, sis, I promise you. I really need you to do this for me, and on top of that, I'll give you five thousand dollars."

Mary held out her hand. "Give me the money, and we got a deal."

"Ain't this a bitch. First, that nigga robbed me, and now my own sister is robbing me." Nut shook his head as he counted out her money.

Mary counted her money twice just to make sure it was correct. "Okay, so now what I gotta do?"

"It's simple." Nut pulled his sister to the side and ran everything down to her.

Two hours later Nut pulled up a block away from a small diner. "A'ight, my peoples said the nigga is in that diner right there. I need you to go in there and get him to meet you later on for a date, and that's it."

Mary sucked her teeth. "What does the nigga look like?"

"He's wearing all-black and a black skully hat," Nut informed her.

"Yeah, a'ight."

Mary stepped in the diner and quickly spotted Gruff sitting over at the counter. She smoothly walked up and took the seat right next to him. She waited for the chef to look her way before she ordered.

"Let me get some home fries, turkey bacon, and some toast." Mary looked over at Gruff's plate. "What's that you got?" she asked.

Gruff answered, "Turkey sausage, cheese, and eggs."

"Damn! That shit look good." Mary asked the chef, "Can I change my order? I want what he got." She looked over at Gruff. "Sorry for being all up in your plate."

"It's all good." Gruff continued to dig into his food.

"You come here a lot?"

"All the time."

"To stay or to go, ma'am?" the chef asked.

"To go please." Mary handed the chef a twenty-dollar bill. "It's this big party tonight," she said, writing down her number. "If you maybe want to go to dinner or something before that, give me a call." She slipped Gruff her number.

"Don't I know you from somewhere?" Gruff said, searching his memory.

"Nah. I just moved out here from Atlanta like four months ago," Mary lied.

"A'ight. What kind of party is it?"

"It's really like a get-together for models, but it's going to be other people there mingling and getting they drink on. I think you'll enjoy yourself."

"Word?" Gruff looked down at her number. "What's your name again?"

Mary said the first thing that came to her mind. "Samantha."

"A'ight, I'ma give you a ring later on." Gruff stuffed her number in his pocket.

"A'ight, I'll see you later."

Mary smiled as she grabbed her food and exited the small diner, and Gruff looked at her ass bounce from side to side until she disappeared out the door.

Tone, laying across the bed watching *SportsCenter*, asked Serena, who was fresh out the shower. "Where you going?"

"I'm about to go pick up."

"You need me to go with you?"

"Nah. You know they be getting all nervous if you come with a new face." Serena stood in front of the mirror butt naked applying lotion to her smooth legs.

"Baby, come here real quick," Tone said, giving Serena a look she knew all too well.

Serena got up on the bed and stood above Tone's face. She purred, "This what you want, daddy?" She then squatted down and began riding Tone's face. She gyrated her hips on his face until she felt herself coming all over his face.

Serena then slid off Tone's face and onto his dick. She pressed down hard on his chest as she bounced her fat ass up and down on Tone's dick.

Tone spread Serena's ass cheeks all the way apart as he plowed in and out of her walls with force. "You love your daddy's dick?" he growled, smacking her ass.

"Oh my God! Yes, I love my daddy's dick!" Serena screamed. She planted her feet on the bed and started bouncing up and down on Tone's dick, forcing him to come earlier than expected.

"Shit! Fuckin' with you got me running late." Serena jumped out the bed and quickly got dressed.

"I love you, baby. Be back in a second." Serena kissed Tone on the cheek, grabbed the moneybag from off the floor, and headed out the door. She pulled out the driveway bumping Alicia Keys' new CD.

Serena pulled up on the side of her Mexican buddy's car so that her driver's side window was right next to the Mexican driver's window.

"You late." The Mexican handed Serena the duffel bag through his window.

"My bad, *papi*." Serena winked as she handed him the moneybag.

"Is everything okay?" the Mexican asked.

"Yes, sir." Serena nodded her head yes.

Just then she saw some flashing lights in her rear-view mirror. "What the fuck!" She screamed as three unmarked cars came to a screeching stop behind her, blocking the Mexican in.

Immediately Serena stepped on the gas and sped down the block.

"Fuck! Fuck! Fuck!" She pulled out her cell phone, quickly found Tone's name, and clicked on it. It rang twice before Tone answered.

"Hey, baby."

"I'm about to go to jail!" Serena said in a fast-paced voice.

Tone sat up. "Huh?"

"As soon as I got the shit, cops came out of nowhere." Serena stopped the car due to the roadblock. "I love you so much, Tone."

An FBI agent roughly snatched her out of the car and threw her down to the ground, where he planted his knee in her back and cuffed her, while several other agents searched her vehicle.

"Hello! Hello!" Tone yelled into the phone. "Mutha-fucka!" He punched the wall.

Tone quickly walked over to his safe and opened it. All the money him and Serena been saving now had to be used for lawyer fees and bail money, if Serena was even granted bail.

"Hello," Mary answered the phone.

"Can I speak to Samantha please?" Gruff asked.

"Speaking." Mary almost forgot that she'd told Gruff that was her name.

"What's good? You trying to grab something to eat before we head out to this party?" Gruff was still trying to figure out where he knew Samantha from.

"Definitely," Mary said excitedly. "For a second, I thought you wasn't going to call."

"Well, I ain't doing shit tonight, so I might as well step out and get some fresh air."

"Sounds good to me. So will you be able to pick me up?"

"If you need me to."

"That would be great. As soon as I hang up, I'm going to text you my address, and I'll see you in an hour."

"A'ight, bet."

As soon as Gruff hung up the phone, something clicked in his head. "Ooooh shit!" he said out loud, remembering Samantha as Yayo's girl. Immediately he pulled out his cell phone and dialed Yayo's number.

"Yo, I was just thinking about you," Yayo answered.

"Yo, you in the crib?"

"Yeah. Why? What's up?" Yayo asked, sensing something was wrong.

"I'm on my way," Gruff said, ending the call.

Thirty minutes later, Yayo heard somebody banging on his front door. He quickly grabbed his .45 and made his way to the door. He looked through the peephole and quickly opened the door.

"Why is you beating on my door like a drum?"

"Yo, is your girl here?" Gruff asked.

"Nah. She at her brother house. Why? What's up?"

Gruff told him, "Hate to be the one to break this to you, but your girl tried to bag me."

"Get the fuck outta here!" Yayo said, waving him off. "C'mon, son, be for real."

"Word to everything," Gruff said seriously. "I'm supposed to be meeting her in thirty minutes."

"You dead ass?"

"Yeah. She looked familiar at first, but I couldn't place where I saw her at before. Then it suddenly came to me."

"You said you suppose to meet her in a half an hour?" Yayo asked, clearly hurt.

"Yeah."

"A'ight, fuck it! I'ma roll with you and confront this bitch."

"You sure you wanna do that?"

"Positive!" Yayo said as headed out the door.

***

Mary, along with Nut and about fifteen armed red-flagged soldiers, sat in the living room of the house she had given Gruff the address to.

"Yo, this shit right here can shoot through cars," a young soldier bragged, loading his machine gun.

"Y'all just better make sure y'all don't shoot me by accident." Mary thought back to the last time she'd listened to her brother and wound up getting shot in her leg.

Nut assured her, "Sis, don't worry about nothing. I got this."

"Yeah, I hope so."

"This the address right here," Gruff said, pulling up in front of the house.

"Call that bitch!" Yayo said, smoking mad.

Gruff pulled out his cell phone and dialed Mary's number and put it on speakerphone.

"Hello," she answered in her sexiest voice.

"Yo, I'm outside."

"Okay, I'm coming out right now."

Gruff looked over at Yayo. "She about to come out now."

"My nigga, don't even get out the car. I got this."

Three minutes later Mary walked out the house looking super-sexy slash slutty.

Before she could make it all the way down the walkway, Yayo hopped out the car. "What the fuck you think you doing, bitch?"

"Baby!" Mary said startled. "What are you doing here?"

"What the fuck are *you* doing here?" Yayo's fist was balled up like he was about to snuff her.

"No, baby, you don't understand!" Mary yelled. "Get out the way!" She was backpedaling as fast as she could in her heels. She heard the door to the house open. She spun around. "NO! WAIT! "

But her words were muffled by the sound of about seven to ten guns going off at the same time. She looked on in horror as Yayo's body got filled with bullets before he hit the ground.

Once Gruff saw the front door swing open and mad niggas come out carrying guns, he immediately put the pedal to the metal. Bullets decorated the passenger side of the car and took out every window in his car.

Mary lay out on the lawn crying her eyes out.

After chasing down Gruff's car for about a block, Nut returned and stood over Yayo's body and emptied six shots from his .38 in his face.

"Noooooo!" Mary cried.

"Come on, sis. We gotta go." Nut dragged his sister over to the getaway van and tossed her inside.

Five blocks away Gruff looked behind him and saw flashing lights. "Muthafuckas!" He said loudly. He only had two realistic choices—Either die or go to jail.

Gruff pulled over his car, and a tear escaped from his eye as he thought about his dog Tiger. He slowly slid out the car with both of his 9s in his hand.

Once the officer saw the man holding the two firearms, he quickly pulled out his .357 and shot Gruff in the neck. Gruff dropped down to his knee, but before he fell face-first into the concrete, he sent two bullets from each of his 9s into the officer's chest, killing him instantly. And Gruff lay on the ground smiling, until all life drained out of his body.

Chapter 20

Santiago sat in his office with a mean look on his face as he talked on the phone. After an hour-long conversation, he slammed down his phone.

"Everything all right, boss?" José asked curiously.

"Serena got busted out in New York with ten kilos," Santiago said in a low tone. "I warned her about fuckin' with those niggas!"

"Ten kilos?" José repeated.

All Santiago could do was shake his head in disgust. "I know that punk-ass boyfriend of hers had her involved in that shit." He banged his fist down on his desk. "I want him dead within the next twenty-four hours!" He looked over at José. "Round up the hit squad and make that nigger disappear!"

"I got you, boss," José said as he exited Santiago's office.

Serena walked in the visiting room and saw Tone over at a table in the corner. "Hey, daddy," she sang as she slid in Tone's arms. "Damn! I fuckin' miss the shit out of you."

"What happened?" Tone asked.

"My father got me a lawyer, and he told me that your father is the one who snitched on me," Serena told him.

"How you know?"

"My father greased a few palms and got some answers."

Tone growled, "I'm going to kill him!"

"He's going to get handled. Don't even worry about it." Serena knew how her father got down.

"How much time they talking about?" Tone asked, scared to hear the answer.

"Forty years."

"Oh, hell naw. "Fuck that! You better tell them that shit was mines. That way, you can do like three years, and I'll take the rest of the time."

"I can do my own time." Serena grabbed Tone's hand.

Tone told her, "Fuck it! If they give you bail, I'm going to bail you out, and we just going to be on the run together."

"Damn! I wanna suck the shit out of your dick right now."

"Did you hear what I just said?"

"Yeah, I heard you, baby." Serena broke down into tears.

"What's wrong, baby?"

"I would love to go on the run with you. But I can't. You have to leave the country."

"Leave the country? Fuck is you talking about?"

"I heard my father has a hit out on you. They are going to kill you at midnight tonight." She started crying some more. "I tried to stop him."

Tone hugged her. "Everything is going to be fine, baby."

"Take that money in the safe and leave as soon as you leave from here."

"Listen, everything is going to be fine. Let's figure out how we can get you up out of here."

"Don't worry about me, baby. You need to save yourself!" Serena stressed. "What are you going to do if you don't leave tonight?"

"Baby, trust me, I'm going to be fine."

Tone smiled, but his eyes told her to pray for him.

"Visiting hours are now over!" the female C.O. announced.

"Daddy, I love you sooooo fuckin' much!" Serena cried as she hugged Tone as tight as she could and slobbed him down. She knew this was probably the last time she would ever see him again.

"Make sure you call me tonight," Tone told her.

"I promise I will, daddy," Serena said as they escorted her into the back. "Leave town tonight."

Tone just sat in his seat and cried as he watched them take Serena away.

After Tone left the jail he went straight to Ice-T's crib. He pulled up in front of Ice-T's house and let the engine die.

Ice-T answered the door and gave Tone a pound, followed by a hug. "Word on the streets is, you a dead man at midnight."

"So I've heard." Tone smirked. "That's why I need that thang."

"I got that for you right here." Ice-T went in his closet and removed a big duffel bag. "Here you go," he said, handing Tone the duffel bag.

Tone removed the M-16 rifle from out of the bag and examined it. "Yeah, I like this shit."

"That's that shit them niggas in the army be having." Ice-T smiled.

"I'll take it." Tone pulled out his money to pay for the gun.

"Keep that," Ice-T told him. "I hope that shit hold you down."

Tone replied quickly, "It will."

"Yo, you need any money or anything to maybe leave the country or anything?"

"Nah, I'm good, but good looking though." Tone gave Ice-T a pound and exited his crib.

Tone tossed the duffel bag in the backseat of his Infiniti before getting on the highway.

Thirty minutes later, he pulled up in front of his father's house. He noticed his father's car wasn't in the driveway, but still he had to just make sure he wasn't home.

He pulled his .45 from his waistband and headed toward the front door. He rang the doorbell five times. Heading back to his car, he still couldn't believe his father was responsible for putting his fiancée in jail for forty years. This was the second time his father had took a woman he loved out of his life.

Tone couldn't help but to cry for the whole ride home. He pulled up in his driveway and let the engine die. He grabbed the duffel bag from the backseat. When Tone stepped foot in his house, it just felt different knowing that Serena wouldn't be walking through that door no time soon. He looked at his watch, and it read 9:30 P.M.

Before he could even make it to the kitchen, he heard the house phone ringing. He quickly rushed over to answer it. "Hello?"

"Hey, baby."

Immediately Serena's voice brought a smile to Tone's face. "Hey, baby."

"It's about time you got home. I been calling every twenty minutes."

"Sorry, baby. I had to go pick up a few things."

"I fuckin' miss the shit outta you," Serena sang into the receiver. "I wanna come home, daddy," she whined.

"I need you home right now," Tone said, feeling his girl's pain. "We will always be together in our hearts."

"I know, daddy. It's just so much I wish we could've done together." Serena's voice cracked.

Tone could hear her crying, but he didn't say anything.

"I mean, why did this shit have to happen to us? We ain't never did nothing to nobody."

"It be like that some time," Tone said.

The operator announced that Serena only had sixty seconds left on her call.

"Well, I guess this is it, huh?" Tone cried silently so Serena couldn't hear him.

"Daddy, I swear I will love you for as long as I live," Serena told him. "You have my heart for life."

"Just know your man is a soldier, and I ain't going out no chump."

"I know that's right, daddy. Better take as many of them mu'fuckas out as you can. I love you, baby, and you have my heart forever," Serena said, just before the phone disconnected.

Tone looked at his digital clock that read 12:04 A.M. He sat at the edge of his bed holding on to his M-16. Just when he thought no one was coming, he heard the lock on his front door get blown off.

BOOM!

Immediately Tone hopped up off his bed and ran toward the top of the steps and aimed his M-16 at the front door and pulled the trigger, dropping three Mexicans. "Come on, muthafucka!" he yelled.

Seconds later, twelve Mexicans ran through the front door yelling something in Spanish as they fired off their Uzis.

Tone waved his M-16 back and forth, hitting ten out of the twelve, dropping them at the doorstep. Tone let his clip drop out the base of his gun as he pulled a fresh clip out of his back pocket and reloaded his gun.

Before he could even finish reloading his gun, he felt a bullet pierce his thigh. "Awww shit!" Tone yelled. He felt his whole right side get numb. The bullet must've hit one of his nerves, causing his whole right side to shut down. "Fuck!"

Tone pulled his .45 from his waist. The first two Mexicans that reached the top of the steps got sent flying straight back down the stairs. Tone was getting ready to fire off another shot until he saw around thirty-five Mexicans rushing up the steps. "Damn!" Tone in a defeated tone. He looked down the barrel of about six AK-47s.

"Fuck y'all niggas!" Tone spat as the Mexicans turned his lights off for good.

Detective Abraham answered his phone, "Yeah, what's up?"

"Have you seen the news?" Maine asked, excited.

"I don't watch the muthafuckin' news." Detective Abraham laughed.

"Tone just got murdered!"

Detective Abraham laughter quickly faded away. "Don't play like that, Maine. That shit ain't funny."

"It's all over the news."

"I'm right around the corner from your crib. I'll be there in a minute." Detective Abraham hung up the phone.

Maine rolled over to the door to let Detective Abraham in. "Shit is all over the fuckin' news." Maine rolled back into the living room.

Detective Abraham sat and listened to the news reporter announce his son's death. "You know that was payback for you getting Serena locked up, right?" Maine said.

"Fuck them Mexicans! They can kiss my ass!" Detective Abraham picked up his ringing cell phone. "Who the fuck is this?"

"Detective Abraham, this is Santiago, Serena's father. I know you heard about what happened to your son tonight. If you don't want the same thing to happen to you, then I suggest you follow these instructions—"

"Fuck you and your instructions! You killed my son!"

"I have a one hundred-man hit team in your city as we speak," Santiago said calmly. "If you want to keep your life, it's going to cost you one million dollars. Leave it in the trunk of your car before sunrise!" Santiago hung up in Detective Abraham's ear.

"Fuck!" Detective Abraham only had $670,000 in the safe in his house. He didn't dare try to run, knowing Santiago had men all over the city just in case he tried to make a quick exit.

"Yo, who was that on the phone?"

Detective Abraham answered quickly, "Nobody."

"That's fucked up what they did to Tone." Maine shook his head. Even though the two wasn't on speaking terms, that was still his friend and former crime partner.

I'ma make them muthafuckas pay for that shit. Detective Abraham sneakily crept up behind Maine and shot him in the back of the head, slumping him over in his wheelchair. "Sorry about that, Maine," he said out loud. "But I need that four hundred grand you sitting on."

He went directly where he knew Maine kept his stash at. "Jackpot!" Detective Abraham smiled as he tossed the two duffel bags over his shoulder and exited Maine's crib. He got in his car and looked at his watch. It read 4:05 A.M. "Fuck!" He stepped on the gas and went flying down the street like a bat out of hell.

Detective Abraham pulled up in front of his house, quickly slid out the car, and ran inside his house to grab the rest of the money.

It took him about thirty minutes to fill up three duffel bags. "Muthafuckin' Mexicans!" he huffed, as he stepped out his house and walked toward his car.

"Don't take another step!" a voice shouted.

Detective Abraham stopped dead in his track when he heard the familiar voice followed by the familiar sound of a gun being cocked.

The voice yelled, "Put the duffel bags on the ground!"

"Don't do nothing stupid. We can talk about this." Detective Abraham turned around slowly and looked the gunman in his eyes. "So this how you gon' do me?"

"Fuck you!" Malcolm shouted. "Payback is a bitch, ain't it?"

"I been nothing but good to you all your life." Detective Abraham smirked. "I taught you how to make money and everything. I even bought you your first car." He saw how filthy and stank Malcolm looked. "But once you got on them drugs, I couldn't fuck with you anymore."

"It's your fault I got hooked on the drugs in the first place! You took my whole life from me, and now I'm about to repay the favor."

"Malcolm, I am still your father!" Detective Abraham yelled.

"Well, you know what they say," Malcolm said, flashing his rotten-tooth smile. "Like father, like son!" He pulled the trigger and watched his father's body drop to the concrete like a sack of potatoes. Malcolm walked over and spat on his father's body as he scooped the three duffel bags up from off the floor. He looked at his father's dead body one last time before hopping in his car and fleeing the scene.

***

The next morning Serena woke up bright and early and ran toward the TV room. Some of the other girls was up watching some bullshit. Serena quickly changed the channel to the news. The other girls huffed and puffed, but nobody wanted to get physical that early in the morning.

Serena's heart sank down to her feet when she heard the news report what happened at her and Tone's home. "Don't worry, daddy. I'ma always hold you down for as long as I live." Serena looked up at the sky, tears rolling down her eyes. "I promise, *we* will always stay strong for you and rep your name," she said, rubbing her stomach.

The End

Notes

Notes

Notes